VIVIANA PRADO-NÚÑEZ

The Art of White Roses

PAPILLOTE PRESS
London and Trafalgar, Dominica

PRAISE FOR THE ART OF WHITE ROSES

"*The Art of White Roses* is a gorgeously written story, full of nuance, sadness, and the joy of growing up. A terrific debut from an exciting new voice in young people's literature."
—Daniel José Older, New York Times bestselling author of the award-winning YA series, *The Shadowshaper Cypher*

"For a young woman's debut novel, Viviana Prado-Núñez writes with startling assurance, eloquence, and beauty. A really promising writer from whom I hope we'll hear a great deal more."
—Jamila Gavin, author of *Coram Boy*, winner of the Whitbread Prize for Children's Book of the Year

"A remarkable story of suffering and hope, beautifully told by an author so young that I can't wait to see what she'll write next."
—Margarita Engle, US Young People's Poet Laureate and Newbery Honor-winning author of *The Surrender Tree*

"*The Art of White Roses* is a luminous coming-of-age story of a young girl and her family navigating the Cuban revolution, bursting with the sounds, scents and terrors of Cuba caught between yearning and loss, between holding onto home and flight. This is a remarkable achievement from a major new talent."
—Diana McCaulay, a 2015 winner of the Burt Award for Caribbean Young Adult Literature

"What wonderfully fresh and youthful Caribbean prose. The teenager Adela grows up fast telling us her story with all the little, ordinary wonders and details of life, and the big things that change everything in her home and on her streets."
—Lawrence Scott, award-winning writer, author of *Witchbroom* and *Leaving by Plane Swimming Back Underwater*

"This book packs a punch—an emotionally engaging storyline that grabs your attention straightaway, richly portrayed characters involved in powerful struggles, and beautiful, lyrical writing that takes your breath away. A novel by a young adult writer to capture the hearts of young adult readers."
—Barbara Bleiman, Education Consultant at the English and Media Centre, UK

Published in Great Britain by Papillote Press in 2018

First self-published by the author in 2016

© Viviana Prado-Núñez 2018

The moral right of Viviana Prado-Núñez to be identified as the author of
this work has been asserted by her in accordance with the Copyright,
Designs and Patents Act, 1988

A CIP catalogue record for this book is available from the British Library

Typeset in Minion

Printed by CPI Group (UK) Ltd, Croydon CR0 4YY

Book cover and design by Andy Dark

ISBN: 978-1-9997768-2-4

Papillote Press
23 Rozel Road
London SW4 0EY
United Kingdom,
and Trafalgar, Dominica
www.papillotepress.co.uk
@papillotepress

Para mi mamá y la abuela que nunca conocí
For my mother and the grandmother I never knew

Cultivo una rosa blanca

Cultivo una rosa blanca,
en julio como en enero,
para el amigo sincero
que me da su mano franca.

Y para el cruel que me arranca
el corazón con que vivo,
cardo ni ortiga cultivo;
cultivo la rosa blanca.

JOSÉ MARTÍ

I Grow a White Rose

I grow a white rose,
in July as in January,
for the sincere friend who
gives me his honest hand.

And for the cruel one who tears
from me the heart with which I live,
thorn nor thistle do I grow;
I grow the white rose.

JOSÉ MARTÍ

(Translation: Viviana Prado-Núñez)

Miguel and the Hotel Nacional

The air must have been quiet, light and fresh the way it never was in the daytime. No gunshots that night. The clouds blocking the sky like a screen door. In the Hotel, a few curtains were open and laughter dribbled out as people held drinks in the windows. They were oblivious. The men in the casino wore tuxedos and the women wore glittery gold dresses that gleamed in the rawness of the light. The others watched television in hotel rooms and their children took baths in rooms lined with tile. Outside, the red roofs were dim in the dark and the trees were twisted as if loving each other. There were cement walkways between them and, though it didn't seem that way, the grass was green and alive.

On one of the walkways was Miguel. It was the end of his shift, and out he came by the staff entrance as the luminescence of the pool shone up to the palm trees. I'd seen pools before in the rich parts of town like Miramar, but this one I pictured special—a hole in the ground five cars wide filled with deep turquoise water. I imagined Miguel with his backpack slung over his shoulder, his good black shoes tied and dangling around his neck as he cut across the courtyard. His feet squelched in the mud and he was having trouble walking.

Then, from behind the brick wall a harsh glow. Headlights. Tyres screeching. A small black shadow against the gloom, lobbed quickly. It landed in the squelch and—BOOM!

His ears, they must've hurt so much. The air probably sucked from his lungs, his head pining for oxygen, his vision shaking. I could imagine the slowness of it. Him raising his head, the mud warm and gooey on his cheek. And, suddenly, all of it going backwards. Rolling, my cousin Miguel rolling, the mud on his elbows like playing baseball in the rain. But slow, so slow, you could see the bits of Hotel grass getting mushed beneath his fingernails.

When he got up, his whole body buzzing with the pounding, the shrapnel must have been scattered all around: a piece in his backpack, the trunk and leaves of a palm tree so decimated he felt like crying. And he did cry, I'm sure of it, though he would always deny it. Right then and there, he cried like a kid and I knew because I saw the tracks on his cheeks when he came back, tracing through the mud.

Tía Carmen was in hysterics.

She'd been that way all evening, and even though she lived a few houses down, she still sat on the couch in our living room, praying under her breath the way nuns at Catholic school did if we used God's name in vain. On most days, Miguel came home by six, and even though he'd said he was going to have a late shift, she'd started panicking at eight. And so, she'd come over from her house with her mascara running and her Bible, making the sign of the cross so many times I thought her arms would fall off.

Tía Carmen was small, with mousy brown hair and creases on her forehead like wrinkled paper. As she sat on our couch and cried, her wrinkles etched themselves deep into her forehead. In the kitchen, Mami stood barefoot by the stove, which was mint-green and smelled of gas. Her hair was dark and she had on a nightgown that needed ironing. She didn't even turn on the radio as she sat cooking,

2

watching a slice of ham sizzle in the saucepan.

Tía Carmen sobbed. "He's dead, disappeared! Gone like Rafi Consuelo. In the dead of night they took him. No note, no explanations—just vanished."

"Carmen, stop it," Mami said. "Don't say things like that. It's bad luck."

"But you know it's true, you know it. When someone goes missing, never seen again! All of them gone! It's already nine o'clock and Miguel's not back yet! *Mi pobre* Miguel, *mi ángel*."

From his big green armchair, Abuelo rolled his eyes. "*Lo juro por Dios*, every time a pin drops, that woman cries."

"*Ay, cállate*, Papá," Mami said.

I stood at the doorway, watching. I wasn't sure whether to be scared or not. Abuelo must have seen an odd expression on my face because he patted the arm of his armchair.

"Come here, Delita."

I sat where he told me like I usually did, leaning into him. I was getting too big for this.

"Don't be scared, Dela," Abuelo told me, "Your Tía is just having another nervous breakdown."

"How do you know?"

"I just do, Dela," Abuelo said. "Trust your *abuelo*, eh? Everything's going to be fine."

Mami pressed down on the ham with a spatula. She lifted it and folded it onto a piece of bread. The spatula wavered in her hand. She didn't look like she thought everything was going to be fine.

"Mami," I said, "where's Papi?"

"*¿Qué?*"

"Papi. Shouldn't he be home by now?"

3

"Yes, well… I'm sure he had some things to tie up at the shop." She sighed as she wet a dishcloth and began wiping down the crumbs from the counter, "Adela, it's getting late. Why don't you go to your room and check on Pingüino?"

Abuelo went back to watching the black-and-white TV. It was a western, but the volume was so low we could still hear Tía Carmen's whimpers. She was rocking back and forth now, murmuring prayers louder than before. I wished he would turn it up.

"*Buenas noches*, Abuelo."

"*Buenas noches*, Adela."

I gave him a kiss on the cheek before leaving.

In my room, time trickled by too slowly. The skinny hand on the clock quivered each time it ticked. Hours passed. I switched on the lamp. There was still no Papi or Miguel. I could hear Tía Carmen's sobs through the walls and it was making me nervous.

It had been one week since the Presidential Palace had been attacked, òne week since Tío Rodrigo had come home from his job as a policeman with his hand wrapped up from punching a man in the face, blood bleeding in speckles through the bandage. Papi had been working downtown in the shoe shop when it happened and he'd said the biggest miracle was that the windows hadn't shattered, that he'd gotten a bunch of strangers running in to cower behind the counters, and that it was a miracle too none of them had tried to rob him. One woman said she'd almost been shot in the head, that the bullet had rebounded off the wall behind her and she'd seen a whole group of people gunned down by police at the corner of Colón and Prado. Meanwhile President Batista had been on the third floor with a gun in one hand and a telephone in the other as people in the streets were getting shot, a man on the radio screaming that Batista was dead

4

even though he wasn't. Afterwards, the tanks had been called in, and even now they crawled over the city like giant green bugs.

I didn't see anything when it happened because I was in school. We'd been pulled out and everything, although I'm not sure why. We didn't live anywhere near the Presidential Palace. We lived in Marianao, a suburb six miles away from Old Havana. By the time we'd gotten home, news of the attack had spread all over the radio. Inside our house, it had been the same then as it was now, except Miguel had been there too. All of us gathered in the living room. Hours passing. Carmen crying, and Mami and Abuelo impassive. Pingüino and I hovering nearby, unsure of what to do, of what calamity to picture. I couldn't remember how Miguel had reacted when he'd heard. He was a blank in my memory. And now he was gone too. And so was Papi.

But this time was different. We'd turned on the radio and the television, we'd checked, and there was nothing. Maybe there was an accident downtown and they were all stuck in traffic. That was what I told myself. But that wouldn't have affected Miguel because Miguel walked home every day, and... I didn't know what to think anymore.

I picked up my journal and started doodling flowers on one of the pages. Pingüino was sprawled out on the bed across from me, asking stupid questions like "Do you think he's dead?" and "Do you think if he's dead, Tío Rodrigo would let me have his baseball bat?"

"Shut up," I told him. "What if he's really dead?"

For a moment, Pingüino was serious. Then he chuckled. "Please. Knowing Miguel, he probably got held back drooling after some *chica* way out of his league."

"You're disgusting, you know that?"

"So are you."

5

I set the journal aside. "So did you do it?"

"What?"

"The lizards."

"Yes."

"What happened?"

Pingüino laughed. "Lots of screaming. The usual."

I rolled my eyes. Everyone knew Pingüino didn't like school, and everyone also knew that he didn't like his new teacher, a young nun named Sister Juana who Pingüino claimed was a know-it-all because she'd gone to some fancy school in America and knew English. So he had taken to playing dumb pranks on her, pranks that weren't even that original. Like putting thumbtacks on her chair, leaving mean graffiti on the chalkboards, and—this time—putting two live lizards in her desk.

"What happens when Mami finds out?" I asked.

"She won't."

I sat up in bed and leaned against the wall. It was humid tonight and the ceiling fan wasn't on yet, so my skin stuck to my shirt and the wall was moist. I squinted at Pingüino's school uniform he hadn't changed out of because he was too lazy. I sighed.

"Where's the letter?"

Pingüino observed the ceiling. "What letter?"

"I'm not stupid, Pingüino. This is the third time, and there's always a letter home the third time around. Where is it?"

"I ripped it."

"*What?*"

"And threw it in a bush. At Rafi Consuelo's house."

"Are you insane? You know not to go there. What if someone had seen you?"

"They didn't. Calm down for God's sake."

I put my face in my hands and watched him through my fingers. "You are dead. When Mami finds out…"

"She won't. Besides, everyone's worrying about Miguel, so no one would've cared anyway. Relax, Adela."

"You can't use Miguel as an excuse. You don't know what's happened to him. He could be dead or lying shot in an alleyway or something. And God knows where Papi is. For all we know they could both be—"

"Can we stop talking about them that way?" Pingüino snapped. "Miguel is fine. He's got to be. And Papi… he probably got held up at work or something."

Fear pulsated in the air. If someone had stalked across the lawn and cracked the window open, they would have heard our hearts beating dull and muted, like the echo of someone tapping their fingers on the other side of a wall.

Midnight. The front door creaking open. A strangled cry from Tía Carmen.

When Pingüino and I got to the living room, Miguel was at the door. His eyes were shattered mirrors. Tío Rodrigo came in and his face sagged from tiredness. He sniffed the air.

"Do you have any food? I'm starving."

The scene could have belonged in a painting. In our living room with its flower print curtains my grandmother made, Tío Rodrigo stood large and hunkering in his blue police uniform, a steady mellow presence like a wall made of concrete. Abuelo sat shrivelled as a prune in his green chair, his glasses glinting in the lamplight. Mami had dragged in the stool from the kitchen and sat with her hands covering her mouth. Pingüino lingered by my side, his hair flat at the back from having lain in the bed staring at the ceiling. He gazed at Miguel as if he were a stranger. On the couch, Tía Carmen smoothed out Miguel's hair and the wrinkles in his clothes and fretted over the grass stains. She was, not surprisingly, in tears. "I'm fine, Mami," Miguel said, scooting away, but his hands shook. "I'm fine." He saw Pingüino and I and smiled, relieved almost.

"Hey, Pingüino. Hey, Adela… The weather's shit, isn't it?"

"Hey, Miguel," Pingüino said, and there was a flicker of a smile. I laughed, but went straight-faced in case that wasn't the right thing to do. When Tío Rodrigo had come home from the attack last week with his hand wrapped up, I hadn't been sure how to react then either. I didn't know whether to say sorry or where to put my eyes or how not to stare, and even now I wasn't sure where to look as Tía Carmen babbled and Miguel dropped his eyes to the floor.

When Mami asked who had done it, Tío Rodrigo claimed it was a couple of rebel kids messing around as usual, but it wasn't anything serious like the Presidential Palace had been. And even though it wasn't much of an explanation, it was enough. Ever since I could remember, the newspapers had had pictures in them of dead bodies riddled with bullets. According to everyone, it was the rebels. It was Fidel Castro's men dying. I didn't pretend to understand much about the rebellion. All I knew was that Fidel was the rebel in Oriente who shot people and Batista was the president in Havana who tortured them. Every so often, there were stories of Batista's blue-helmeted police who plucked people off the streets and tortured them for days on end, or shot down an entire family and left a survivor to keep the fear going. They liked to march through the city in rows, guns aloft, blue uniforms crisp like their mothers had ironed them that

8

morning. Then in the countryside there were rumours of rebel boys with guns hiding in trees and picking people off from afar. But it was hard knowing what the truth was because everyone knew the newspapers were lying. I couldn't tell who was right or wrong in this thing. I guess Batista was bad because everybody said so and Castro… No one was sure about Castro.

Everyone said those boys in Oriente would fail. It was inevitable. Batista had been in power much too long for things to change. No matter how many pictures in the newspaper showed Batista walking through crowds of Cubans weeping at his feet, kissing babies in their mothers' arms, riding in the passenger side of an open-roofed car with his shining canine smile, everyone knew hell would freeze over before Batista gave up being president, before anything in Cuba changed. But no one said any of that in the open. People wore the fear on their faces when they walked on the street, when they went to the grocery store. They jumped when an engine backfired. No one would ever talk because it might mean being the next corpse in the newspaper.

"Everything is okay. Whoever did this, we'll catch them," Tío Rodrigo said. He gazed at Miguel and Tía Carmen on the couch. "I promise."

After Tío Rodrigo had eaten his fill and Tía Carmen had calmed herself down, they went home. From the window, I watched them walk towards their house. I stayed there a while, gazing at the empty street, the way the streetlights made everything mysterious, the way the humidity drifted in through the window. Straining my eyes, waiting for the glint of the hood on Papi's car, watching Tío Rodrigo's hunched back round the corner. And I wondered, I couldn't help wondering, about how many things Tío Rodrigo had lied about.

2.

The Other Adela

That night, I woke up at three in the morning in a cold sweat. I had had a dream about a bearded rebel who shot Papi and Miguel at the Hotel Nacional. In the background, Tío Rodrigo watched from a police car parked underneath a palm tree, Batista smiling his canine smile in the back seat.

It was a gunshot night. I could hear them pop-pop-popping in the distance, long moments of silence in between, and then a sudden spurt of violence punctuating the air. I observed Pingüino's sleeping form, envious, and listened to his steady breathing. I jiggled my foot under the covers, waiting to fall back asleep, but every time I closed my eyes, another round would start up again and it would sound as if it were closer this time. I tried remembering what the rebel's face had looked like in the dream, but I couldn't. I could only remember a blob of colour with the mouth moving.

I didn't mean to, but I started imagining the gunshots as a horde of rebels with blurry faces coming closer and closer to our house in Marianao, flooding up the street past Miguel's house, barging through the front door with their guns drawn. I couldn't imagine the details of what would happen next. I knew somehow it would end with people dead on the floor, but I couldn't picture it, I didn't want to. I decided I didn't want to imagine anything any longer.

When I trudged into the living room, the light from the black-

and-white TV was washing over everything, making it all gray and ghostly. Abuelo sat on the couch, his green armchair deserted in the corner. There was no one else, but he was smushed right up against the arm nearest to the television, leaving the rest of the couch vast and empty like he was waiting for more people to join him.

He raised his head.

"I had a bad dream."

Abuelo didn't speak. Instead, he patted the place next to him, and I curled up against his side. His clothes smelled of tobacco and coconut water the way they always did. There was another western on and I watched it with my eyelids drooping, pretending the gunshots in the distance were coming from the television. On the dresser were the family pictures: Mami when she was a little girl on a pink tricycle with streamers. Mami and Papi's wedding day, and them on the front stairs of our house in Marianao. Me as a toddler peering over at baby Pingüino in his crib. Papi's big plantation family lined up for a portrait in front of the sugarcane fields. The *abuela* I was named after, smiling next to the mango trees a few months before she died of cancer.

I was born three days after Abuela Adela died, and the way Abuelo told it, it was like a miracle when I came because I had her green eyes and dark blonde hair. He hadn't been sure what that meant, but he thought they should name me after her because of it. And they did. But my eyes weren't a pretty green like characters in books. They were muddy like pond water—a green you mistook for brown until you looked more closely. My hair was alright. It wasn't a bright blonde like the *americanas* in films, but it wasn't my Mami's hair either, black and rippling. It was an in-between like my eyes, something no one could put their finger on.

11

Not that anyone ever noticed me anyway. No one in my class ever spoke to me, except maybe to ask me to move a few feet over to make room for a baseball game. While they were playing, I always imagined myself dissolving into walls, my skin camouflaging into the colour of bricks, leaving behind hovering eyes and a mouth. The only friend at school I'd ever had was this impossibly tiny girl named Elena in the first grade who had had the same last name as me, so she used to follow me around and call me her sister. She transferred to another school soon after, so I ended up alone again pretty quickly. But that was okay. I had Miguel and Pingüino when I went home. And during recess, I had the journal I drew pictures in and the tree in the courtyard whose roots made a seat for me almost like a pair of intertwining fingers.

Still, I wished I could talk to people, or that people would talk to me. Maybe if I looked different, if I were prettier, if I weren't so plain, people might pay more attention, maybe that would be enough. I wondered sometimes if Abuela Adela had ever felt that way, but I suppose I would never know. It was far too late for that. But if she'd gotten someone like Abuelo to fall in love with her, I suppose she must have had something extra, something more I hadn't been born with. I didn't believe in ghosts, but when I was smaller, I used to imagine she was hovering nearby, listening to my thoughts, wanting to give me advice, but staying inevitably silent. Then I stopped imagining because I thought people should only imagine ghosts if they believed in them.

There was no one else who was thirteen and lonely. Or maybe there was and no one talked about it. The other kids didn't like thinking. They liked cursing when the nuns weren't listening and calling each other *pingas*. They liked ignoring the rebellion and buying sugar-crumbled *churros* from the black man with the cart who sold them after school. I just did my schoolwork and then came home and listened to Miguel and Pingüino annoying each other while people claimed the world was falling apart. I didn't feel like the world was falling apart though. I felt more like I was floating, trying to keep track of where was up and where was down and feeling very wrong sometimes. And all the while I tried not to imagine the dead grandmother I was named after floating nearby and smiling bittersweetly.

"Abuelo, do you miss her?"

He tore his eyes from the television and gazed at the picture of her on the dresser. In it, she was still beautiful: lips plump, teeth in a crescent moon, eyes piercing through the black-and-white. She hadn't become skin-and-bones yet. She was happy.

"All the time, Delita." He stroked my hair. "All the time."

That was the great thing about Abuelo. He didn't ask questions, only answered them. He let you put your head in his lap, stroked your hair until you fell asleep, and didn't say a word.

The Strange Disappearance
of Rafi Consuelo and Anita Valle

The disappearance of Rafi Consuelo was a neighbourhood mystery. It had happened around three weeks ago, like Tía Carmen had said, in the dead of night. The only witness was Don Manolo, the old man who lived on the corner across the street from Miguel, smack-dab in the middle of the intersection. It was two o'clock in the morning and he was outside on his porch, smoking a cigar after having been woken by the barking of a faraway dog.

Don Manolo lived alone, in the house nearest to Havana on the east side, and on that night, the sky was windless and sweeping. He saw a sleek black car drive down the street and park itself on the curb in front of Rafi Consuelo's house. He remembered noticing it because it was a nice car and nice cars weren't something you saw outside of the city, unless it was going to the cabaret or the racetrack nearby.

But there it was. It had stopped right there and soon enough, he heard a resounding knock. Then Rafi Consuelo answered this strange man in the night.

Rafi Consuelo was new to the street. He was young, somewhere in his twenties, and had moved into his house last November after the rebels closed the University of Havana. He was nice enough, and average-looking. He often offered to referee baseball games when he saw groups of kids heading to the small grassy field near the school. When he was a kid growing up in Havana, he'd said, he used to be the best pitcher on his street, but he messed up his throwing hand doing fisherman's work for his father. Everyone always turned him down. And the one time he'd offered me a carton of orange juice from his front porch because his fridge had stopped working, I turned him down too. Because even though he was young and nice and we saw him hanging out sometimes with the police officers on their lunch breaks, he was a stranger, and we'd heard enough stories about kids being found dead in the streets.

It seemed to Don Manolo, on that night, that Rafi Consuelo and the man were arguing, because he saw them waving their hands around a lot. Despite how far away they were, he could still hear a faint sliver of their voices floating out into the open air. He didn't hear what they'd said, but he could tell they were talking, and they were angry. Eventually, the man persuaded Rafi Consuelo to get into his big black shiny car, and off they went speeding into the darkness.

Don Manolo didn't think much of it until Rafi Consuelo didn't come back the next day. Or the next. Or the day after that.

His house was dim and barren, all the lights off, the broken fridge on its side in the front yard where he'd left it. Every time someone from the neighbourhood walked by, they craned their heads and tried peeking into the windows.

Everyone had their theories. Pingüino said he'd been abducted by a mobster because he owed him money, and now he was as good as dead. Miguel said he was off getting laid somewhere, the lucky bastard, but I didn't think so. Papi thought rebels as usual. Abuelo didn't know and didn't care. He said he wasn't even sure how Rafi Consuelo had got onto our street in the first place: how does a student with no money, no parents or relatives to speak of, end up living in a house on his own? There was something suspicious about that, Abuelo thought. As for me, I didn't like guessing.

No one dared mention the police until the second person went missing. Anita Valle, another former University of Havana student, nineteen years old. She was a pretty, flat-chested black girl who'd babysat Pingüino and I around a year ago. She was known around the neighbourhood for her first-rate brain, and the shy way she used to go to school every morning with her head down like she could feel people watching her through the windows. Because they were. Because even though everyone knew Anita Valle was the smartest person on our street, everyone also knew the Valles were the poorest.

Like the rest of Marianao, they hadn't made it past secondary school, they worked menial jobs. Doña Paula was a maid at one of the rich people's houses, and if you happened to be up early enough in the morning, you could see her starting the nearly two-hour walk to Vedado in a pressed gray dress and plain black shoes. Don Álvarez, meanwhile, could be seen even on the hottest summer days selling crates of bananas, mangoes, and watermelons from the red-and-yellow cart he bicycled all the way to the intersection near the cabaret, a cardboard sign with the prices misspelled dangling on the side. Their house was an unpainted shack that stood half-broken at the end of the road, the garage abandoned in open air, held up by columns without walls. Inside you could see bits of furniture with the cushions missing, Doña Paula's tarnished sewing machine on the floor, dead leaves, and Don Álvarez's banana cart parked in the centre with the paint flecking off in metal bits and pieces.

Anita Valle was their chance at a way out, and everybody knew it. It wasn't often Marianao produced girls who got straight A's, especially when those girls lived in houses with the walls missing. She was the only one anybody could picture getting a good enough score on the entrance exam for the University of Havana to get in, and to go for free—other than Luis Rodríguez, the fidgety son of our family friend Doña Theresa who lived a couple of doors down. His intelligence had come as a shock to everyone when he'd got in too, but before that, it had been Anita Valle and Anita Valle only that anybody expected to make it out of here.

She was alright as a babysitter, but she wasn't the best cook. She could make *arroz con pollo* faster than anyone I knew, in under twenty-five minutes—but she didn't know how to season *por ningún carajo*, and before dinner I often found myself sneaking in garlic when she wasn't looking so that it would at least taste like something. I didn't mind though. She brought us *mamoncillos* when she picked us up from school and helped with our maths homework when we didn't know how to do it, and on those nights it would almost feel like school was worth something.

Even Miguel used to come over before he dropped out and they would sit together at the kitchen table, Miguel cracking jokes as he tried to get her to do the problems for him ("*Dale*, Anita, *por favor*, it's not like I'm passing anyway, I might as well get some of it right…"). And she would smile in that way of hers, brush a stray strand behind her ear, and tell him if he wanted it he had better work for it. "*Sí, Señora, como no*," Miguel would say, grinning in that stupid way of his, tipping an imaginary top hat in her direction. Then she'd roll her eyes, hand him a fresh sheet of paper, tell him to start over again.

But just because school was a way out for Anita Valle didn't mean it was a way out for the rest of us. Pingüino didn't get good grades and neither did Miguel. School was a place to mess around with friends if you had them, the place we happened to walk to and come back home again from every day. And maybe at some point it could've been a way out for me too because I was good at it, but the University was closed now. No one knew when it would reopen or if it ever would, and I couldn't afford to go anywhere else. And so I was a story repeating itself. A familiar one I imagined was being told all over Havana. But still, back then there had been the hope, and that hope had been Anita Valle.

There were no witnesses the night she disappeared. The only person who said he'd seen anything was her little brother, Diego, who was ten, the same age as Pingüino. He said he'd been half-asleep when he saw it, but he swore he knew it was her—his older sister Anita Valle sneaking out of her room at night, fully clothed. And a few seconds later the hinges on the door creaking, closed shut in a way that made him think she was trying to be quiet.

Gone. Just like Rafi Consuelo in the middle of the night.

The night-whispers. Papi and Mami in the kitchen and me hunched outside the doorway, watching their shadows move on the floor.

What if it's Batista? That car—what if it was the police? What if there's a rat? But that's crazy. Maybe in Havana or Oriente. But not here. Not our street. Not Marianao. Please not Marianao, don't let there be a rat here, please not here…

Tío Rodrigo had informed his bosses of both disappearances, but he told us there was nothing he could do. They had told him not to worry. He told us to keep quiet, to not panic, to keep the peace.

But in the middle of the night-whispers, I heard Mami, the trepidation in her voice.

¿Y Rodrigo?… You don't think…?

4.

La Mañana Después

The next morning, I walked into the living room and Papi was tangled in a bundle of blankets on the couch. Mami stood over him, livid.

"Where were you?" she said.

"I told you, Deianeira, I had to work."

"Don't give me that shit. Miguel almost blown up at the Hotel, Carmen over here in hysterics, and there I was half-scared to death. And after last week, don't even try telling me I'm exaggerating because I'm not. Where were you?"

"*Ay*, Deianeira, *por favor—*"

"Papi?"

Mami turned towards the window. Papi attempted a smile, his hair a fuzzy mess at the top of his head.

"*Hola*, Dela," Papi said. "Are you ready for school?"

"Yes. But Pingüino's still sleeping. Also your hair's messed up."

Papi ran a hand through it and chuckled. "I don't know what you were expecting, Dela. I just woke up."

"Adela, get your brother up, please," Mami said, ignoring him, "I'm walking you to school today."

"You are?"

"*Sí, mija*. So get moving, *arranca*."

Ten minutes later and we were walking out into the humidity.

Outside, Don Manolo sat on his front steps reading the newspaper as a few dogs snaked in and out of the allamanda bush of yellow flowers that separated his house and Rafi Consuelo's. He waved when he saw us and we waved back.

Marianao wasn't the prettiest to look at. The roads were cracked, speckled, and gravelly and the power lines sagged with the palms. The sidewalks were so battered and broken-up in places that it was easier to walk in the gutter or on the street or on a wayward patch of grass. On the parts of the street where the jungle ran wild alongside it, there were bits and pieces of garbage like tyres and stray shoes. There was a beach a few minutes away, but the sand was grainy and the sea rough despite being the right shade of green. In the Plaza, there was a big marble statue in the centre and if it weren't for the people and the butcher shop, it could've passed for being respectable. But the whole place stunk of blood and meat, and beggars stooped at the curbs.

Our street wasn't like that so we never strayed far. I loved our house especially. It was small—one storey high with a concrete porch and blue walls on the outside. In the back, we had a yard cramped with mango trees because Papi's father used to own a sugarcane plantation and Papi's favourite thing about it had been the small batch of mango trees near the front door. His parents were all dead and now, it was Tía Noelia, her husband, and her four kids who ran the place in Oriente. We'd never been because it was on the other side of the island near the Sierra Maestra, the mountains where all the rebels were supposed to be.

The Valles' house was almost as lifeless as Rafi Consuelo's, and I saw Mami glancing back at it and its drawn shutters before heading further down the street. Mami was wearing her faded flower print dress, the yellow one she wore when she didn't feel like thinking about what to wear. It was ugly and smelled of oldness and no one knew where it came from.

"Stand up straight," Mami told me, "You look like an old man."

Mami used to be a dancer. She loved ballet and I remember once when Papi happened to have a little money lying around, he took her to the theatre in Havana to see *Swan Lake* around Christmastime. It was the only time I had ever seen her get ready for anything, the only time I'd seen her use the old dressing table that had belonged to my grandmother.

She'd sat there for hours with all the brushes and the paints and dabbed them on like an artist in front of the mirror, which was ornate and silver and so glamorous it could have belonged in a palace in France. I had been fascinated by her lipstick especially, red and shining and sticking to her teeth when she didn't notice, but I loved it anyway.

"Mami, I don't want to go to school," Pingüino said all of a sudden. "The nuns are mean and boring. Diego's cousin, Armando, doesn't go to school and he's just fine."

"Diego's family is poor and it's a miracle they can read, much less that they could send Anita Valle to college. You should be grateful. *Ahora cállate, mijo.*"

"*¿Y* Miguel? Miguel doesn't go to school."

"Miguel has a job."

"*Pero* Mami—"

"*Dios mío, qué mucho tú jodes,*" Mami threw her hands in the air. "Why don't you talk about something else? Look at Adela, I never hear her complaining. Why can't you be more like her?"

Pingüino knew better than to talk back. Mami was in a mood. The

21

kind where she might not be mad at you, but she was mad about something, and talking to her was a surefire way to get yelled at or smacked around unnecessarily. We walked in silence a while before I asked the question I'd been thinking about since I'd seen Papi on the couch in the bundle of blankets.

"Mami, where was Papi last night?"

Mami pretended like she hadn't heard. Pingüino adjusted his bag as he walked.

"Mami, where do you think—?"

"*Oye*, it's Luis," Mami said, "*Hola*, Luis!"

Luis Rodríguez stood on the other side of the street. Mami went to hug him, and he hugged her back, looking very uncomfortable. When she let him go, he lingered at the side of the road like he didn't know what to do with himself. Luis resembled his mother a bit around the eyes. He had that old soul look, the kind that made you think he was wise beyond his years. He was only in his twenties, but he looked like he was older. I didn't think he was very handsome. His ears stuck out too much, he had an awkward black moustache, and he seemed perpetually nervous, adjusting his glasses to make sure they weren't slipping. His shirt was a battlefield of old stains and he wore khakis that looked like they hadn't been washed in a few weeks.

"*Hola*, Doña Deianeira," Luis said.

"Luis, I thought you were away."

"I came back early. Have you seen Rafi?"

"Didn't you hear?"

"Hear? About what?"

"Rafi's gone."

"Gone?"

"Disappeared. A car took him away in the middle of the night. Anita's gone too."

"What?" Luis's face had gone pale, like he'd eaten a bad *arroz con leche*.

"Your mother didn't tell you?"

"I just got back. What about the police? Have they said anything?"

"There's been no news, but you know how they are. How's your mother? I haven't talked to her in a while."

"She's fine, she's good—Do they know how it happened?"

"Like I said, a car picked up Rafi in the middle of the night and he hasn't been back since. And Anita's little brother says he saw her sneaking out, but they think she was taken too. And that's all we know. *Pero mira*—tell your mother I haven't seen her in a while, and she should come by sometime. And you too, of course."

"Yes, that sounds…Can you excuse me a moment? I need to go."

Luis's eyes were shifting, panicky, like those of the dog who'd been run over two years ago near the house. It had happened overnight. A taxi filled with drunken tourists heading back from the cabaret had run over one of the stray dogs on our street. We woke up to the whimpering and the yowling the next morning, the dog lying with its ribs crushed at the foot of Abuelo's car near our house. I remember Miguel, Pingüino, and me standing over the body, Pingüino wondering if he should touch it, and the dog's eyes rolling and flashing, like someone flipping the channels on the television too fast.

Mami looked perturbed. "Luis, are you okay?"

"Yes, yes, I'm fine. It was nice seeing you, Doña Deianeira. *Buenos días*." He stumbled off. We walked on. I glanced back once to watch him, and he eyed the street before sneaking into his own house, two houses down from our own. A small coral house with a pristine white rocking chair in the front, fit for an American grandmother, and a clump of lemon trees in the back.

Pingüino giggled. "He looked drunk as hell."

Mami smacked Pingüino in the arm.

"*¡Ay!* What was that for?"

"Watch your language, Pingüino, I mean it."

"What? But I didn't even—!"

Mami sighed and gazed toward the sky as if asking God for patience. But it was more than that. For a moment I thought I saw sadness. Like when a breeze went by and the petals of a flower moved so limply they seemed defeated. But like always, it melted away when she thought someone was watching. She smiled in a faltering way.

"I think you two can make it from here on your own." She kissed us both on the forehead before leaving, waving goodbye at the corner where we could no longer see her, her tired yellow dress fluttering limply in the breeze.

5.

Con la Mano Derecha

Sister Tula was one of those nuns that liked the ruler. It was a long one and the wood left red marks an inch wide on the wrists. It bent before it hit, then snapped—*smack-smack-smack*. The whole class winced.

I didn't get the ruler much, but the girl next to me, María Viramontes, got it all the time. She was left-handed, which was a problem, because according to Sister Tula, "All God's children use their right hands." María was a nice girl with a soft, round face, but she cried easily. When the tears started streaming and her face went red, Sister Tula got even madder. "*¿Eres estúpida o qué?*" And she'd smack her again.

We didn't learn much in school. We wore uniforms and socks that itched at our ankles. We sat at our desks and sweltered in the heat as the teacher wrote Bible verses on the board. We tried not to drop things on the floor while Sister Tula was speaking, because then she might get angry and hit us with the ruler.

When Sister Tula got to talking about God, it was easy to get bored. Sometimes she talked for an hour and I became fixated on the palm tree that drooped by the window. If it was nice outside, the fronds swayed a little and you could hear the whoosh of it through the walls. But if it was raining, you could see the raindrops plunking onto the leaves.

There were also the mornings when we "prayed for penance". An hour a day, kneeling on rice grains, praying to God to forgive us for our sins. The rice was oblong and hard and embedded itself into our skin. By the end of it, there were dots on the underside of our knees and rice grains sticking like ticks to our legs. When it was time to go to class, the rice grains detached themselves and made a trail down the hallway.

It was raining today and we were writing paragraphs about José Martí, a Cuban revolutionary who fought against Spain and got himself shot on the first day of battle. I didn't like him very much. The picture of him in the textbook reminded me of Luis Rodríguez because of his stuck-up ears and black moustache. Except José Martí was even uglier—he was skinny as a scarecrow and his hairline stopped way at the top of his head and his moustache was so big it was like a giant furry butterfly had landed on his lips. The things he wrote were nice, but they were the expected things about liberty and fighting for what you believed in. It was hard imagining him starting a revolution or leading troops into battle. I was thinking about José Martí's moustache and how it might fit onto Pingüino's face when Sister Tula's voice interrupted.

"María, how many times have I told you? You write *con la mano derecha.*"

Smack-smack-smack.

María cried by the teacher's desk. Sister Tula glowered from behind her glasses. María mumbled something and her voice was fogged over with tears.

"What was that? What did you say? Speak up." The ruler wavered in Sister Tula's hands.

"I—I said that José Martí was left-handed."

26

"What?"

"My Papi told me I was different because I was left-handed, and that José Martí was different too."

I figured María would get smacked again because that was what usually happened. Instead, Sister Tula was bewildered for a moment before she said, "Back to your seat." The class watched in astonishment as María was set free. She walked to her desk, eyes on the floor. Her hair hung and covered her face. As she settled into the seat next to me, I heard her trying to sob in a way that was quiet.

Outside, the palm tree was drooping.

The rain plunked and the leaves shuddered behind her.

6.

Con la Mano Izquierda

Abuelo's car smelled like cigars, whiskey, and *agua de coco*. It was a blue the colour of hard candy and if you squinted a little, it could've been a gangster car. It was mostly Papi who drove it into Havana to work at the shoe shop, but we called it Abuelo's car because Abuelo was too stubborn to think of it any other away. He won it off a guy— *un italiano*—in the casino long before I was born and it had been his ever since. For all I knew, it could've been nice before, but these days, it was old and battered and the wheels were rusted like old bicycles that had been left out in the rain. Whiskey with *agua de coco* was Abuelo's favourite drink and whenever he decided to go for a drive, it was Pingüino who was stuck making it for him. That rarely happened, but even so, there was still an empty glass in the front seat next to Papi and it smelled of alcohol.

As we drove into Havana, I gazed out the windows, at the chaos of it all. What I loved about it most were the people. There were old ladies smoking cigars on the sidewalk and girls with their skirts cinched who giggled at the young men. In the streets, the old men peered over the balconies at the boys Pingüino's age who played baseball with their shirts off.

And the buildings, of course—I'd never been to Spain, but that must have been what it was like. The cathedrals, the castles, el Malecón by the sea. In the older part of the city where Papi worked, the buildings were crumbly and beautiful. Some had huge red domes and others were colonial houses with large glinting windows. The streets were lined with rugged cobblestone and dirt-specked buildings that popped with colour every few blocks—tangerine, bright turquoise, pink, lizard green. Alleyways turned into staircases with shops on the side, their signs hanging over the streets in mid-air. In the newer part, the buildings were different. They were white and tall like pillars of salt in the sun. The streets were filled with people and fancy cars and cyclists with fresh produce in their baskets and vendors at the stoplights who sold guavas, *guapén*, mangoes, *plátanos*, flowers, and miniature Cuban flags.

The tanks were leaving the city as we drove in and we had to stop at an intersection as one of them rolled by, huge and green, the cannon sticking out like an eyestalk. Pingüino had never seen a tank and he was fascinated, staring with his mouth agape, nudging me and saying, "It's so *big*, Adela." When the tank passed, we drove on. Traffic in Havana was never-ending and we drove with the windows down so that the honking drifted in, the curse words lazing about in the air.

I was leery about being in the car with Papi. The last time he'd driven us to the shoe shop after school, he kept bothering Pingüino about the nine-year-old girl in his class named Lucía and saying that he'd seen Pingüino making goo-goo eyes at her in church and that he had asked Mami to organize the wedding already. Pingüino kept hitting him on the shoulder every time he said something stupid, but Pingüino laughed anyway because Papi could make things funny even when they weren't. Until we stopped at an intersection and there was a girl with a short skirt and high heels walking at the curb. It was obvious she was a prostitute. You saw them more in the alleyways in groups, but rarely alone. She was thin, but her shirt was up to her navel and her skin hung out a bit at the back. Then the light turned green and Papi and Pingüino were laughing about girls and Papi said, "Hey, look at this one." He rolled down the window and yelled "*¡PUTA!*" as he drove around the corner. It was only a split second, but I would never forget the expression on the girl's face as she spun around to see who had called her a whore. It was the same as María's when Sister Tula smacked her in the front of the classroom. In the end, she was a girl. Just like me and Lucía and poor María Viramontes. I knew she was a prostitute, but I couldn't help feeling sorry for her anyway. For a while afterwards it was hard seeing Papi, the same man who had taught me to ride a bike and to write my name in cursive, without seeing the girl's face and the slight 'o' of her mouth and the question in her eyes as he raced away from her roaring with laughter.

"Listen," Papi said from the front seat. "I'm taking you both to work because Mami is helping Doña Theresa with something. You know the rules. If a customer comes in, be respectful and then come and get me or Dulce."

Pingüino and I nodded. Papi ran a hand through his hair. Pingüino fiddled with his fingers, tapped them on his knees, because Pingüino could never keep still.

"Papi," I said. "Was José Martí left-handed?"

"I don't know. Why?"

"Because María got smacked with the ruler for writing with her left hand, and she said José Martí was different and left-handed."

"Different, maybe, but I don't know about left-handed. This girl got smacked for that?"

"Sister Tula says God's children only use their right hands."

Papi shook his head in the mirror. "*Qué mierda.*"

"I don't get it," I said. "Was she saying José Martí was bad?"

"What do you mean?"

"He died on the first day of fighting. He failed."

"That doesn't make him bad, it makes him imperfect. And José Martí didn't fail."

"Yes he did, he—"

"I don't like José Martí," Pingüino said. "His head is a weird shape. And so is his moustache."

"He looks like Luis Rodríguez," I said.

Pingüino laughed and Papi sighed. "You both should have more respect. José Martí was a deep thinker and a great poet."

Pingüino wrinkled his nose. "What?"

"You read poetry?" I said.

"Ew," Pingüino said.

"I read his. Don't you know *Cultivo una rosa blanca*?"

"Is that part of *Guantanamera*?" I asked.

"A part of it is, but... You really haven't heard of it?" We stared at him through the rearview mirror. Papi cleared his throat:

"I grow a white rose,
in July as in January,
for the sincere friend who
gives me his honest hand.

And for the cruel one who tears
from me the heart with which I live,
thorn nor thistle do I grow;
I grow the white rose."

"...But what does that mean?" Pingüino said.

"Think about it," Papi said.

"I get it, I think. But I don't understand," I said.

"That's okay, Dela," Papi said, gazing out the side window. "White roses are hard sometimes."

His head became very still, so still it might have been made of wax. Even the droplets on the front window moved more than he did. Out the side window, there was a little boy, hardly older than Pingüino, with his ribs sticking skinny from his bare chest like a washboard. His face was smeared with dirt and he sat at the curb with bare feet, watching our car go by. It was like he'd been sitting there for ages, waiting for our car. The top of his shirt was wet from the recent rain. It wasn't long before he disappeared in the blur of dirty buildings, and the occasional weed sticking up defiantly from the ground. Then the whiteness of the Havana buildings took his place, as if the ugliness had never existed.

Papi put his eyes back on the road. "White roses are hard for me too."

7.

At the Zapatería de Cuba

The shoe shop in Old Havana was run-down and ugly-looking on the outside. The paint was green and peeling from the walls and the golden letters of Zapatería de Cuba were fading into dust. That wasn't to say the inside wasn't run-down and ugly-looking too. Papi tended to be disorganized, so his workbench in the back was strewn with old shoes and bits of people's soles and loose shoelaces. Lining the walls were boxes and boxes of shoes—loafers and solid-coloured high heels and old lady sandals made of leather. The whole place reeked of it, really. Walking in was one long, warm gust of leather.

Papi inherited the business from Abuelo. He was never meant to run the shoe shop, but when Mami got pregnant with me in college, there wasn't much else to be done. At the time, he was studying to be a lawyer and Mami was studying to be a nurse like Abuela Adela, but then both of them dropped out. I'm not sure if Abuelo ever approved, but I know he wished Mami had finished school. When we were sitting together in the living room watching the black-and-white TV, he would say, "All that money I saved to put her through college, the least she could do is finish." That was what Abuelo did most of the day—complain. And when he wasn't complaining about some ache or pain, he was sitting on the couch watching television or listening to *Radio Reloj*, the local radio station.

I sometimes thought about being a lawyer or a nurse, about being the things people should have become before life got in the way. But I didn't know if I liked those things. The only thing I guess I liked was drawing, but I'd seen what an artist's life in Havana was like. It was little old men and women on stoops by tourist sites begging Americans for portraits or selling skylines of Havana made up of blots of paint like parrots' feathers, and I didn't know if I wanted that. I hardly knew what I wanted anyway. Besides, there wasn't much point in dreaming. Not when there were bills to pay and school uniforms to save money for and cars to fill up on gas.

The shoe shop was the reason Papi took Abuelo's car every day. He didn't make enough money for us to pay tuition for Catholic school and to have a black-and-white TV and a whole other list of things. Most of our money came from the plantation, and a distant uncle of Mami's in America who was a lawyer. Papi didn't like this uncle, I could tell, because every time he got an envelope filled with cash, he'd stare at it with such hatred, I wondered why he even took his money at all.

He would never tell me why he hated Mami's uncle so much, but I assumed it was because he was an American. Papi really hated them. He ranted about them every day, about how they were the reason for the drugs, and the prostitutes, and the casinos. They were the reason Havana was dangerous, the reason for the poverty. If you walked a little way down the street, you saw the kids on the sidewalks and their mothers with their skirts stained. And it was all the Americans' fault, according to Papi. We were lucky, he said. Very lucky. But the truth was I didn't need him to tell me that. It didn't take much to remind you how lucky you were.

When we walked in, there was that gust of leather air in our faces and Dulce at her desk. As far as I knew, you didn't need a receptionist to run a shoe shop, but Dulce had found ways to make herself useful. Mostly she sat there and looked bored, but every once in a while she would get a terrific spurt of energy and organize the place. You'd walk in and it would be unrecognizable—Papi's trinkets and things on the workbench sorted into sections, and the boxes clean and dusted and perfectly arranged by size and whether they were men's, women's, or children's. And Dulce would be standing on a chair trying to get the duster on the very tippy-top shelf with her tongue sticking out. Then when customers came in, she would be smiley-faced and boisterous, complimenting the women as they tried on shoes ("*Esos sí que están monos*. Would you like them in another colour?") or subtly touching men on the arm as she gestured them towards the loafers section ("We've just had a brand new shipment—handmade. *Así que no te preocupes por la calidad*"). I often tried picturing myself doing what she did, but I wasn't sure I could do it. I wasn't sure I could speak to people that way. But Papi liked talking about how I might have to do Dulce's job when I grew up, so I didn't know if I had much of a choice.

As we went to put our stuff down, there was a customer talking to Dulce at her desk and when Papi saw her, he froze. She was skinny and dark-skinned, like she was part black for sure, and she had on a tight, knee-length skirt with a slit that left her legs exposed to the open air. They were pretty girl legs, but sweating slightly because it was hot in the shoe shop and we only had the one fan. She had a pair of old red flamenco shoes in her hands. On the desk was the box where she'd got them from, and the tissue paper was unfurled across the surface. I realized I'd seen her before hanging around the shop, but I couldn't pinpoint when or what her name was. She wore lipstick, like Mami when she was going out, except it wasn't as nice somehow. And she had lots of eye makeup, clunky and bristly on her eyelashes. Her top was worn and fuzzy, and it went off her shoulders. She had a beauty mark above her upper lip, like singers on the television.

"How much?" she asked Dulce about the shoes.

"*Treinta*," Dulce said, and the girl sighed.

"It's a shame. They're beautiful."

"They're a bit old though. What about those other ones?"

"No, it wouldn't be the same."

"Well, it's too bad you can't have them…" Dulce turned from her. When she saw us, she grinned. "*Hola*, Don Sebastián. *Hola*, Pingüino. *Hola*, Adela. *¿Qué pasa chica?*"

"*Nada.*"

"*¿Y tu*, Pingüino? How was school?"

"Fine," Pingüino said sullenly. "I got detention again."

"*¿Otra vez?*" Papi said, looking at him. "Are you joking?"

Pingüino shrunk into a corner. "You're not going to tell Mami, are you?"

I thought Papi was going to hit him upside the head, but Dulce intervened, "*Ay*, don't be too hard on him, Don Sebastián. We all mess up sometimes. Right, Pingüino?"

Pingüino nodded, glancing back and forth between Dulce and Papi. The girl Dulce had been talking to lingered behind her.

"This is my sister, Celia," Dulce said, introducing her. "She'll be leaving soon, don't worry."

"Are you the shop owner?" Celia asked Papi, stepping forward.

"Yes," Papi said.

"Is there any way I can get these shoes for a lesser price? I really do want them."

"No, I'm sorry. I could perhaps find you something similar in the back."

"But I don't want something similar. I want these."

"Celia!" Dulce hissed.

"Well, I do," Celia snapped, "Is it so terrible to want something you can't have? But that's just the way with things. Isn't it, Don Sebastían?"

Papi blinked. "I—"

"That's enough, Celia," Dulce said. "Why are you here? It's not the shoes, it never is."

"What's that supposed to mean?"

"There's always more. You wouldn't be here if there wasn't more."

"You think I want money, don't you?"

Dulce's eyes flicked towards Papi. "I never said that, I just think—"

Celia shoved the shoes back into the box with the tissue paper and there was a sound of crumpling. We watched without speaking. She marched back to the mishmash of what may have been, at some point, the women's section, and placed the box on top of a mountain of mismatched Mary Janes. She turned around.

"Can I talk to you?" she said, looking at Papi.

"Me?" Papi said.

"Him?" Dulce said, "Why?"

"Yes, him. And none of your business."

Papi saw Pingüino and me standing there with our school stuff weighing us down, and didn't know what to do.

"Why don't the both of you do your homework in the back?"

Pingüino and I stared at him. The one thing Papi never did was ask us to do our homework. Pingüino shrugged, "Okay." He shuffled away, clueless.

As I walked by, I attempted to pick out Dulce's features in Celia's face other than the skin colour. There wasn't much resemblance, except for maybe the nose. She met my eyes and I felt embarrassed for having stared at her, but I was struck by how desperate she was about her red shoes and her need to want them.

I was almost to the back door when I heard Papi whisper something: "You need to leave. We'll talk later." Celia was about to protest, but Papi forced her out the door. Celia stumbled and caught herself. She walked away and glanced at Papi once through the window before melding into the sidewalk. Before I knew it, she was gone.

8.

Los Americanos

Los americanos who came to the Hotel Nacional, Miguel had once told us, were all the colour of milk and had skinny butts and fancy bags made of leather. I'd told him I didn't really care what they looked like, but the pool—what was the pool like? The pool, he'd said, was a giant concrete bathtub people scraped their toes against if they weren't careful, and the water had so much chlorine it made people's hair squeak when they got out afterwards. The colour was blue. Kind of like the shallow part of the sea, but less greenish, less kind. It was more fake, more glow-in-the-dark. But those American women, Miguel had said. *Coño*, were they cute. Their bathing suits were cut perfect for their bodies and they were always trying to get their milk-skin to bronze. But all that happened was their cheeks got too pink like undercooked meat.

And the mobsters? Pingüino had asked. Did they keep their guns with them at the pool?

No, of course not, Miguel had said. But they were real macho, real scary. They kept their girls nearby and smoked so many cigars that the ashtrays were strewn with burnt logs like a forest had burned to the ground. And they wore these gold chains around their necks… in the *pool—en la piscina*.

We no longer talked about it that way. *Los americanos* weren't funny anymore. They were bizarre bloated entities gazing at us over a large chasm, blinking their eyes in the distance and staring without understanding much of anything. At least that was the way Miguel made it sound.

When he'd first started working there, there had been a glamour to it, a kind of mystery—the Hotel Nacional was the biggest building in Vedado with white walls and tall red roofs and rows of palm trees that lined the road where the rich people's cars and taxis drove down. When he talked about what happened on the inside, we used to hang on every word. But these days Miguel's job at the Hotel Nacional was just that to him—a job. It was where he folded towels and listened to *gringos* massacre Spanish and dance dumbly in the dark while smoking the cigars they liked so much. He hadn't had much to say about it in a while. Until now.

After we got back from the shoe shop, Miguel was lounging on the second step of the porch waiting for us, twirling a piece of grass between his fingertips. We gathered around him like schoolchildren, and Papi had barely closed the front door behind him for three seconds before Pingüino began berating him with questions.

"Does Tío know who planted the bomb?"

"No."

"How loud was it, do you think?"

"Well, I couldn't hear for a while afterwards."

"Did anybody die?"

"No, *estúpido*. It was in the papers. No one was hurt."

"Was it cool, like in a movie?"

"Depends what you mean by cool."

"Were you scared? Did you cry?"

Miguel quit twirling the piece of grass in his hands. "Well—"

"I bet you cried, didn't you? Are you—?"

"*Dios mío*, Pingüino, let him breathe," I said.

Miguel shrugged, and let the piece of grass fall to the ground. "It's fine."

"So is everything alright at the Hotel now?" I asked.

"The bomb didn't do much. The shrapnel got scattered around, but that was it. It didn't land near anything important... I mean, except me."

"But did you cry though?" Pingüino asked.

"No, Pingüino, I didn't cry!" Miguel yelled. "Although I'm sure you would've, you little wuss."

"I am not a wuss. And I bet you did cry, but you're too chicken to admit it. You're scared even now."

Miguel tried laughing it off, but it didn't work. I thought of the dry trail of tears down his cheeks the night before.

"Everyone's scared, Pingüino," I said. "Especially with what's happened to Rafi and Anita."

Pingüino scoffed. "I'm not scared. I went over to Rafi Consuelo's house just the other day, and there was nothing to be afraid of."

"Yes, there was. Mami if she caught you."

I explained to Miguel about the letter Pingüino's school had sent home because of what Pingüino had done with the lizards and Miguel laughed. Pingüino crossed his arms. "Like you're not scared either, Adela. You can't even walk by Rafi Consuelo's house without trembling. Don't pretend like I haven't seen you."

"That's because I'm not a *comemierda*. Like you."

Pingüino stuck his tongue out and I ignored him.

"Are you still going to work there?" I asked Miguel.

"It's not like I have much of a choice."

"You could try finding another job."

"Somehow I doubt another bomb is going to get thrown at me, Adela. I think I'll be fine."

"Or you could go back to school."

"*Ay Dios no.*"

"School is terrible," Pingüino said. "The only reason I go is because Mami makes me."

I rolled my eyes. "*Por favor*, Pingüino, you don't even know what you're talking about."

"I do too!"

"Oh? Give me one good reason why you shouldn't go to school anymore."

"Because I don't belong there."

"What do you mean?"

"I mean. I'm stupider than the other kids. I think. That's what people say."

"Who says that?"

Pingüino looked at his shoes. "Teachers. They say I don't do good in school. And I always get detention. They don't like me."

"That's because you do stupid things, that doesn't mean—"

"It doesn't matter, Adela. I don't like school. But that's okay. Because one day I'm gonna be a racecar driver and have more money than the President. *Y después todo el mundo se puede ir pal carajo.*"

Miguel laughed.

"Mami said not to curse," I said.

Pingüino rolled his eyes. "I don't understand what the big deal is! Mami and Papi curse all the time!"

"You're a kid, it's different."

"I bet if you cursed, Mami and Papi wouldn't care."

"I don't do it around them so…"

"That's not fair."

"Who ever said anything was fair?"

Pingüino opened his mouth, decided against it, and gazed at his shoes again. I thought of the brick wall at school where I pictured myself dissolving. I thought about how when I sat in the tree's roots in the courtyard, I would glance up from my journal sometimes and watch the other kids play. I imagined my face looked something like the way Pingüino's did now.

I sighed. "Fine. You can curse. Just not around adults."

Pingüino looked up, a huge grin on his face. "Really?"

I laughed. "Yes, really."

"You won't tell?"

"No."

"Awesome."

"You're both so immature," Miguel said.

"*Mira quién habla*—you're the one who dropped out," Pingüino said, still grinning like an idiot.

"You're right. I hated school," Miguel said. "But that doesn't mean I'm anywhere near as much of a kid as you two."

"You didn't seem to hate school when Anita Valle was around," I said.

"What?"

"Don't you remember? When Anita used to help us with our homework?"

"Yeah. She used to give me candy when I got things right. She was nice," Pingüino said.

Miguel stared.

"I don't know," I said. "School was fun back then, wasn't it? Because she'd get you to understand things. I like understanding things."

Miguel shifted uncomfortably. "I guess."

Pingüino's smile faded. "I miss her," he said.

"I miss her too," I said.

More silence.

"I wonder where she is right now," Pingüino said.

"Don't—" Miguel started. He shook his head. "That's not a nice thing to wonder."

"What? Why?" I said.

"Because I've been around bombs and stuff now, and knowing how afraid you can be when you think you're going to die… And she's been gone for weeks and I can't imagine… Well, that's the thing I *can* imagine it and I *have*… And it's not fair because she was such a… It's just—it's not good to think about those things, Adela."

Pingüino and I stared at him.

"You know she didn't want me to drop out," he said.

"What?"

"Anita. I told her I was going to drop out and she didn't want me to."

"When was this?"

"One night. The night Tío Sebastían took Tía Deianeira out to see some show or something. So they got home early and she was about to leave. I told her and she had this whole long talk with me about why I shouldn't do it."

"But you dropped out anyway."

"Yep. Now I work at the Hotel. Which is bad, but in a different way. Like today there was this big fat tomato of a *gringo* in the restaurant with his big fat tomato family saying things about how *wonderful* the beach was and how *wonderful* the food was if only the people weren't poor and making things ugly. And I was really tempted to quit, I was. Because I don't understand how they can look at us and think we're ugly. But I didn't."

"*Los americanos son extraños*," I said. "Papi says it's all their fault. Maybe they don't know it yet."

"You know," Miguel said. "I thought she would've been disappointed. When I dropped out. But I didn't see her much after that. I used to wonder if I'd talked to her again, what she would've said. And now I'm working at the Hotel and I wonder what things might've been like if I…" Miguel paused before speaking. "She was a good person," he said simply.

Miguel's voice quavered near the end and before he even spoke, I saw the lights go off behind Pingüino's eyes, but it happened too fast for me to stop it.

"*Oye*, Miguel's crying! Adela, do you see it? He's crying!"

"Pingüino, shut up," I said, watching Miguel's face. There were no tears, but a dangerous kind of blankness.

"*Sí*, Pingüino," Miguel said in a deadly voice, "*Cállate la jodía boca o te la rompo.*"

Pingüino laughed and chanted, "*Miiiguel's a chiiiicken, Miiiguel's a chiiiicken.*"

"SHUT UP," Miguel yelled, and he pushed Pingüino off the porch onto the ground. He would've started punching him, but I got up and grabbed him by the shoulders.

"Miguel, no! Stop it!"

"*¡Dale, cabrón!*" he screamed at Pingüino. "Call me one more thing, I dare you! Go on! Do it!"

"Pingüino," I said, holding Miguel back, "Don't you d—"

"*Maricón*," Pingüino shouted.

And then I was on the ground too, but I didn't have time to think because Miguel was punching Pingüino and Pingüino had begun to cry and that's when the screen door opened and Papi emerged shirtless from the house.

"¡OYE! ¿Qué está pasando aquí?"

Miguel scrambled away from Pingüino and Pingüino sat up, gulping tears. They faced away from each other, neither answering.

Papi turned to me. "Adela?"

"They were… they started fighting."

Papi turned back to them. "No more fighting. Whatever happened, it's over. Pingüino, *por favor*, stop crying or it'll upset your mother. Miguel, it's almost six o'clock. You should probably head home. Carmen will be worried."

"Sure thing, Tío," Miguel said, catching his breath and standing back up again. "No problem."

Pingüino wiped his face with his shirt and it came away with blood. He sniffled. Papi paid him no mind.

"*Adiós, primos*," Miguel told us. He glanced at Pingüino and almost seemed sorry.

"Goodbye, Miguel," I said. Pingüino stayed silent, tears streaming down his face.

Miguel walked down the street and disappeared at the corner. Papi walked back in. I went to help Pingüino up, but he pushed me away and went snivelling into the house. After a couple of moments, I followed.

I thought about *los americanos*. I thought about the ones Miguel had mentioned with the luggage made of leather. I thought about the women who sunned themselves by the pool and the big fat tomato *gringo* with his big fat tomato family. I wondered if they knew about everything. About the poverty and the torture and the fact most people couldn't read. About people like Miguel who dropped out of school and ended up unhappy with their lives anyway, folding towels and talking to kids on front porches every day. About all the stories they would never know because they looked at us—at these people who got into fights about the way others cried, who lived in small blue houses and sold shoes on the weekdays—and thought of us as ugly. But perhaps it was hard knowing something was your fault if you were stuck on the other side of a chasm, if you were cocooned inside the Hotel Nacional with its concrete-bathtub pool and its palm-tree-lined roadways and its tall red roofs. Perhaps that was the world to them. Perhaps they would never know my world and I would never know theirs. Perhaps they were doomed to be witnesses who witnessed nothing at all. Perhaps it was better that way.

9

Doña Theresa and the Lemon Trees

Sometimes, if we knocked on her front door and said *por favor*, she let me and Pingüino pick lemons from the trees that grew scraggly in her backyard. Which was exactly what we did on Saturday morning. Luckily, it wasn't raining and she let us in. Mami said Doña Theresa was only forty, but she didn't seem that way. She was like an *abuela* with wrinkles around her eyes, mouth, and hands, which were covered in small brown freckles. When she smiled, you could almost imagine she was beautiful once.

Pingüino and I, we came prepared. We armed ourselves with the white bucket Mami used to clean the floors and long-sleeved shirts for leaning deep into the branches. Doña Theresa's lemon trees grew along the back fence and were wild and crazed. The lemons weren't ready so most of them were green, except for those few that grew yellow and plump way in the back. Because Pingüino was so little, I had to hold onto the back of his shirt when he leaned in to grab one. It was slow and hot and soon there were sweat stains on the pits of our lemon-picking shirts.

"Hey, Pingüino," I said as I held him by the shirt.

"Mmm-hmm?"

"Where's Luis?"

"Does it matter?"

"I don't know. I was just wondering."

"Don't mention it then. Can't you see I'm concentrating here? *¡Carajo!*" The lemon he'd been pulling at ripped free and plummeted through the brambles. It fell to an indiscernible part of ground, most likely near the fence.

"Pingüino!"

"Sorry."

"That's the fifth one! *¡Mira lo que estás haciendo, cabrón!*"

"You keep distracting me. And I thought you said not to curse around adults. Do you want Doña Theresa to hear?"

I readjusted my grip. My hands were sweaty and my fingers hurt. "No… But you cursed just now."

"Well, I'm not anymore." He quietened down as he set his sights on another lemon, this one fatter than the last. It was closer than the other one had been, but we'd missed it because it was curtained in a tangle of leaves and thin, scratchy branches. It was so close I saw the pores on its skin.

"Ooh. Get that one. That one's good."

"*Shhht.*"

He leaned forward. My fingers tightened on his shirt. A drop of sweat tickled my brow. I wiped it away. Pingüino reached his arm through the gaps in the tangle of branches. His fingers brushed the bright yellow peel and—

"Hey, Pingüino," I said before I could stop myself.

Pingüino jumped and the humongous lemon he had just plucked fumbled from his fingers. It made a ruckus as it smashed to the ground and rolled to the back where, once again, we could not reach.

"*¡ME-CAGO-EN-LA-PUTA-MADRE-QUE-TE-PARIÓ-PERRA-CABRONA!*" he screamed.

The back door of Doña Theresa's coral house swung open and

Doña Theresa stood in the doorway, smoking a cigarette in a pink nightgown and bare feet. I let go of Pingüino. He lost his balance and almost crashed into the lemon trees.

"*Niños*. I hope I didn't hear what I think I heard."

"It was Adela, Doña Theresa," Pingüino said. My jaw dropped.

Doña Theresa sighed. "I don't doubt it. Most children curse when they think their parents aren't listening. It's one of those things everyone knows, but no one talks about."

Doña Theresa took another drag of her cigarette before waving the smoke at us. "Hurry up and pick those lemons so I can squeeze them. That's what you came for, isn't it?"

We nodded.

When we had filled up a third of the bucket, Doña Theresa made her lemonade, which was better even than Abuelo's. Pingüino and I sat at the counter in front of the fan, elbowing each other for room. Doña Theresa's kitchen was small and rickety, a thin streak of rust lining the spot where the sink ended and the blue-and-white wallpaper began. As I watched Doña Theresa press the lemon husks into the juicer with her hands wrinkled like an *abuela*'s, I thought of Luis again.

"Doña Theresa, where's Luis?"

"What?" she said, not taking her eyes off the juicer.

"Luis. Where is he?"

"I don't know." She sighed as she threw a shrivelled lemon husk into the sink. "I hardly know what that boy does anymore."

The fringes of Doña Theresa's pink nightgown were frayed and there were burn marks on the skirt. If I concentrated, I could see the crests of her nipples poking through. I didn't think Doña Theresa ever wore a bra and I wondered if she had ever worn a bra, even when she was young. I wondered if I would need a bra soon. I hoped so. I didn't want to end up flat-chested like Anita Valle. I wasn't sure why being flat-chested was such a bad thing, but from the way Miguel talked, if I didn't want to end up dying alone, I probably should pray for some breasts.

The front door opened.

"Luis, is that you?"

"*Sí,* Mamá." He walked into the kitchen and his ears stuck out as prominently as ever. He really did look like José Martí.

"Oh good. I was just making some lemonade for Adela and Pingüino. Do you want some?"

"Adela and Pingüino?"

"Yes. The two Santiago kids."

He blinked as if he didn't recognize us. "Two of them?"

"Yes. There's another one. Their cousin Miguel, remember? You used to play with him when you were little."

"Oh."

"Are you okay, *corazón*?"

"*Sí,* Mamá, I—" Luis took an uncertain step forward. He was about to say something and changed his mind. He stepped back.

"…I'm sorry."

He rushed down the hallway and I was surprised at how fast Doña Theresa went after him.

"Luis, come back."

"No, Mamá."

"At least have some lemonade."

"No, Mamá. I don't want any."

The door slammed as Luis retreated to his room. Doña Theresa screamed. "If you won't tell me what's wrong, at least tell me what I can do to help. Luis? Luis?"

We waited for the silence to end, to hear Doña Theresa's muffled footsteps come back down the hall, to have her pour the lemonade and pretend as if nothing had happened. Instead, we heard the sound of stifled sobs, quiet and gasping. I got up from the stool, the legs scraping loudly against the floor, and Pingüino followed. We found Doña Theresa crying in the hallway, hugging herself so hard she made finger marks on her own arms. She sat on the ground, her knees drawn up to her chest, not caring if her underwear showed.

"Doña Theresa?" Pingüino asked. "Are you okay?"

Doña Theresa sniffled and wiped her nose with her hand. "Of course, I'm okay. I'm always okay. Adults are supposed to be okay, aren't they? Maybe you two should go now."

"What about the lemonade?" Pingüino asked.

I stomped on his foot.

"*¡Ay!*"

"What's wrong with you?" I hissed.

"No, it's all right," Doña Theresa said, blowing hair out of her face. She picked herself off the ground and wiped the tears from her cheeks. "I promised lemonade, and lemonade I will give."

We stayed as silent as we could as she finished pressing the husks into the juicer, flinching every time she was done with a lemon and threw it into the sink with a loud bang. By the end of it, lemon juice had squirted onto the ceiling, onto the linoleum, onto the blue-and-white of the wallpaper. She gave a shuddery breath as she poured the lemon juice into two glasses along with some water and sugar. She mixed it with two silver spoons so old they had speckles on the hilt. I didn't complain.

"Run along," she said as she gave it to us, spoons and all. I watched the bits of translucent pulp settle to the bottom. "Bring back the glasses and spoons the next time you're over here."

"*Sí*, Doña Theresa. We will. I hope you feel better," I said, before she could usher us out the door.

She nodded. Her nightgown had lemon juice on it, right over her left nipple. I pretended not to notice.

10.

Mami in the Kitchen Making Ropa Vieja

The walls were the colour of oranges and when the sun came up, it was blinding. Mami and Papi didn't have much money when they first moved in, but Mami had made sure the kitchen was one of the rooms painted because she'd known it would be where she'd be spending the most time with the garlic cloves, the bags of white rice, the tins of olive oil in the pantry.

Mami loved cooking to music. She always put her hair in a ponytail before stretching to turn on the radio next to the refrigerator. When she was happy, it was Celia Cruz and she mamboed by herself as she stirred *picadillo* in the pan and plopped in the red peppers. When she was sad, she might not cook at all, but Frank Sinatra played as she sat at the stool and leaned her elbows on the table. In the mornings, it was *Radio Reloj* and she smiled as she asked Pingüino and I what we wanted for breakfast.

What I really loved was when she made *ropa vieja*. On Sundays, she woke me up before the sun rose. I tried nudging Pingüino awake too, but he would groan and put a pillow over his head. So it was just Mami and me next to the kitchen sink in the moonlight. I helped her shred the beef and the juice stained my fingertips. It was quiet, except for the breeze and birdsong that drifted in through the open window, rustling Mami's hair and mine too. Then, we put the beef in the copper pot with the garlic, the peppers, the onions, the spice, and the olive oil from the tins.

Today, the beef was cold and dank on my skin. Both of us had a plateful and we shredded it in silence as Mami's fingers moved without thinking—slender fingers tanned more on the outside than in. I studied my own and found them pale the whole way around, the way none of my family's fingers were except mine. Mami broke the silence.

"Have I ever told you about the costumes?"

Mami's eyes were at the window, and they were cracked with silver.

"What costumes?"

"The costumes from when I danced."

"No."

"I wish you could have seen them. They were made out of this silk that glowed. We were only ever dressed in white. I never knew why."

I shrugged. "Maybe because it's nicer. Like…" I thought of José Martí. "Like white roses."

Mami gazed out the window. "I used to pretend they were wedding dresses. That there were flowers in my hair because I was getting married… That's where my wedding dress came from."

"What?"

"My wedding dress. It was an old ballet costume."

I thought of the wedding picture in the living room, the one I had passed by every morning on the way to school, every night Abuelo and I sat together and watched television. I had never thought to ask about the dress, had presumed it was tucked away in a corner of the house in a big box with a bow on it.

"Why?"

"Your grandmother had sold hers and we couldn't afford a new one."

"Oh."

"Sometimes…" Mami was pained, trying to find the words. Her fingers continued tearing. I believed she would be tearing forever, trying to find the words. "Sometimes… I wish things had turned out differently."

Her words hung heavy in the air. I could see a stray gray hair streaking out above her head. No one spoke, and we continued on, the only sound of strings of meat being ripped apart. We gazed into the dimness, a single house with its lights a faraway square in the dark. Mami tensed beside me. I recognized the sagging front porch, the broken refrigerator on the lawn, the windows that had been dead for weeks. I caught my breath.

It was Rafi Consuelo's house.

"Mami," I said, and my voice shook.

"I know, Dela, I see it too."

We stared. And just as suddenly as the lights came on, they went out with a black finality.

"Mami—"

She let out a breath. "Don't talk about what we've seen, Adela."

"Okay, but—"

"Don't worry about it. I'll take care of it, *mija*." She tucked a yellow strand behind my ear. "I always do."

We went back to shredding the meat, and I snuck peeks out the window at Rafi Consuelo's house, wondering if anyone had seen the lights too, trying to discern the slightest brightness behind the closed shutters. But there was nothing. Mami and I were silent. I could feel her watching me every time my eyes wandered to that dead house down the street.

I knew things would proceed as they did most Sundays. We would go to church. Papi would wear his good dress shirt and the shoes he had shined himself that morning. Abuelo and Pingüino would trail behind, grumbling. And the *ropa vieja* would be stewing in the pot all day until we returned, the aroma seeping its way around the house until dinnertime when Mami cracked the lid open.

With the steam billowing and everyone—even Abuelo—gathered around the pot, her eyes would be satisfied. The same way she would have looked, I imagined, if she'd become a nurse like she was supposed to, if it weren't for me.

11.

Flies and Prayers

I didn't like church much, but I didn't say it out loud, especially not at school where Sister Tula could hear. Abuelo hated church the most, which I didn't understand because I thought old people were supposed to be more religious. Abuelo had stopped praying when my grandmother passed away. He said he only prayed nowadays when he thought it was worth it. On our walk to church that morning, I wondered if he had prayed at all for Rafi Consuelo and Anita Valle in the last few weeks. But as much as I wanted to, I couldn't picture Abuelo getting on his knees by his bedside with his head lowered. He didn't seem the type.

The lights of Rafi Consuelo's house were off as we passed it.

"Strange…" I said.

"What's strange?" Pingüino asked. In front of us, Mami slowed, listening.

I whispered it in Pingüino's ear. "I'll tell you later."

To me, churches were supposed to be tall with arches and towers and a big bell on top someone had to climb a staircase to get to. I wanted my church to have cobblestone on the outside and marble steps that gleamed even when it wasn't raining. I wanted one of the old Spanish churches in Havana that I went into once with Papi to light a candle at the foot of the *la Virgen María*. I remembered everything gilded in gold, and paintings of saints, and stained glass that

58

made the floors glow with triangles of colour. I remembered the way footsteps echoed, and the ceiling so high it was as if the walls were growing all around us. Like I'd turn away one moment and come back the next and the place would be a whole world taller.

Instead, I got our ratty church in Marianao. It was a cream colour on the outside, with flecks of grit on the walls from years of cars splashing puddles onto them. The windows didn't open because the latches were rusted shut and it took two grown men to get them open. So most of the time we had Masses with the door open, and hoped for a stray breeze because no one had the money to donate an extra fan. It got hot in there quick, and while sitting in the pews, you'd see women who sweat so much they brought their own handkerchiefs to wipe their faces. The only decoration was a simple wooden cross at the front, and the altar with its tablecloth and cheap golden trim. If you got up closer, you could see the thread was loose on one side and sticking up like a stray hair.

Mami, Papi, Pingüino, and I slid into a pew while Abuelo sat at the aisle. In front of us were Tía Carmen and Miguel and every once in a while Tía Carmen stroked Miguel's hair before placing her hand on his shoulder. Don Manolo sat behind us and I could hear him clearing his throat in that way of his, like he was permanently clogged. On the opposite side of the church, Anita Valle's little brother, Diego, swung his feet and stared at his fingers. His mother and father were huddled next to him. Behind them were Doña Theresa and Luis, Luis fidgeting as he zoned out at the back of Diego Valle's head. At the back wall of the church, Tío Rodrigo leaned with his arms crossed, waiting for Mass to start.

Padre Francisco entered from a side door. He was small and portly, with wispy gray hair around a bald spot that shone in the heat. I liked

Padre Francisco. He let me and Pingüino come around twice for communion crackers even though he knew we did it only for the food. When he mentioned things from the Bible, I didn't pay attention much. When I was little, I would try to understand what he was saying but I never could. I felt like I was faking it when he asked us to pray. I was faking believing in God, in Jesus, in saints. They would always be nothing more than decorations on the inside of pretty Spanish churches in Havana.

But sometimes there were moments when I wished for something more, moments when I was tired of the way I ached for the things I couldn't name. It would catch me in flashes—during a lull of boredom at school, or in the middle of watching someone else's eyes as they talked, or walking alone around Havana trying to smell the sea in the wind and inhaling nothing but air. I wanted so badly for there to be a God, an entity spread across the sky who would reach out a hand and fix everything, rock me to sleep on those nights I felt so lonely I wanted to curl into myself and never wake up. But that was only sometimes and I wasn't sure sometimes was enough.

"I have had many of you coming to me," Padre Francisco was saying, "asking where God has gone. What has He done with our children? What has He done with our parents, our brothers, our sisters? Why does He take some and leave others behind? How can we watch this go on and on and do nothing but pray? You've asked me these questions and you continue to ask them, and every time I struggle with how to answer you. And perhaps I could pretend to know the answers, but I will not do that because it is my job to be truthful and I will not deceive you. Instead, I will tell the truth and the truth is this: I cannot tell you what will become of us. I cannot tell you what will become of Rafi Consuelo or Anita Valle or their families. I cannot tell you what will happen tomorrow or next week or next year or even within the next decade. For God is not someone we demand things of, but someone we open ourselves to in order to reach the end of our paths, whatever those paths may be. And the assumption that we are doing nothing by gathering together and praying and hoping and thinking is a dangerous one. The insides of our minds are more powerful than we think. I refuse to believe that the act of prayer, of retaining the missing within our minds and refusing to let these details of our lives become unimportant is a futile one. I know that openness is one of the hardest things I can ask of you right now. I know this is a time in which we may not want to hear about belief.

"But let me tell you what I believe—what I truly, sincerely believe. I believe that one day at the penultimate moment of our lives, we will look back. We will remember this little church in Marianao, and the people who gathered in its pews, and how small we all felt, and how high we had to rise. We will remember how hard it was to keep ourselves aloft, how hard it was to believe that that was enough. And we will be grateful that we did so. So grateful we will want to fall to our knees in gratitude for the strength God gave us. So I ask of you now to bow down in prayer even though I have asked it of you so many times before. I ask of you now to hope just as much as you have done every time before this even though it may pain you. Pray for us, for yourselves, for others. Pray for those who are lost, for those who have been left behind, and for those who have been saved."

Mami reached for Papi's hand. He took hers into his own and kissed it, a crease appearing at his chin. If I leaned forward, I could see Abuelo's fingers gathered in his lap, wrinkled and unmoving. Pingüino's eyes were concentrating on a fly that pinged against the ceiling near a cobweb. Everyone bowed their heads, and Pingüino hurried to follow. I decided I would try even though I never did, except for the few times I had felt desperate enough to kneel at my bedside while Pingüino was sleeping. Maybe this time God would listen. I closed my eyes, and drowned out the noises—Pingüino shifting next to me, Don Manolo's resonating cough, Mami's sniffles as she tried not to cry. My neck was warm and there were goosebumps on my arms.

…Please please please let them be alive, let them all be alive. Don't let them be dead. I don't want them to be dead. I want those lights in Rafi Consuelo's house to be Rafi Consuelo and I want Anita back teaching us maths and making *arroz con pollo* without enough seasoning. I want them back, *Dios, por favor, devuélvelos*. Give them back, please. Thank you for Miguel, I need him, I don't know what I would do if he… Please help us. Please. Help Mami love herself again. Please be real, I want you to be real…

I opened my eyes and glanced around the room, feeling self-conscious as I closed my eyes one more time… And God? Some breasts wouldn't hurt either. Thanks. Amen.

People prayed and their mouths moved as they whispered. It wasn't long before everyone was finished and Padre Francisco resumed Mass. I watched the stray golden thread that stuck up from the end of the altar's tablecloth. Even though I had prayed, I still felt like there was something missing. I had felt no presence in the air above me. I still felt like I was alone. Maybe I hadn't believed as hard as Padre Francisco had needed me to. From behind us, a shadow blocked the sun streaming in from the open door. I turned and so did Pingüino.

Two men I had never seen before. Both young, both tan, and both with wisps of beards. Their clothes were grungy and green and stiff as if they'd been sweat in a long time ago. They slipped into the last pew on the other side of the church. Tío Rodrigo stood by the back wall, and he narrowed his eyes as they walked past him. Mami poked me and Pingüino in the shoulders when she saw we weren't paying attention.

We turned back around. The fly had stopped pinging against the wall. It was caught in the gossamer web, a small black dot writhing.

12.
The Two Strangers

At the end of Mass, Papi, Mami, Abuelo, Don Manolo, and the Valles filed up to Padre Francisco at the front. The people in the church idled out to the food on the lawn. I watched as Diego Valle took the hand of Lucía from a few streets over. She swung a rag doll and her eyes gazed wetly upwards as she stumbled by. Tío Rodrigo waited at the end of the aisle for Tía Carmen, and they walked out together. From the other side of the church, I saw her pursing her lips as Miguel and Pingüino lingered by the pews.

"This can't go on any longer," Don Manolo was saying at the front, "We can't wait for someone else to be kidnapped and the police are useless. We need to do something."

"Don't be stupid. There's nothing we can do," Papi said, and Mami frowned. "Unless you want to get us all killed. Or arrested. Or worse."

"I bet it's those rebels," Don Manolo spat. "Or the police. If you ask me they're all in on it together, trying to make our lives a living hell. I say we—"

"What?" Papi said. "Protest? Arm ourselves? It's all been done before. It's happening now and it doesn't do anything, except get more people hurt. There's never anything anyone can do. That's the way this works."

"No," Mami said. "There's always something we can do. The trouble is figuring out where to start."

"What are you suggesting?" Don Manolo said.

"Nothing," Mami said, blinking. "It's much too dangerous anyway."

"Padre Francisco, what do you think?" Abuelo said.

"Honestly…" Padre Francisco sighed and rubbed his scalp. "I think for now maybe we should let the police handle this. See if they come up with anything new."

"They won't," Don Manolo insisted, "They won't because they don't want to. When has anyone official in this country ever told the truth? I've been alive for nearly eighty years and I've never seen it. Not once. There are people missing, Padre. This can't go on."

"That's what they all say," Papi said darkly.

"I don't care about any of that," Doña Paula said. "I don't care. Padre—" Her voice broke. "I want my daughter back. Even if it's just a body."

They all went quiet, and Don Álvarez shifted where he stood. I tried to imagine Mami and Papi sad that way, wishing my body would show up somewhere, in a ravine, by a roadside, anywhere— as long as they could throw me a funeral. Doña Paula opened her mouth to speak, but couldn't. Padre Francisco hugged her.

"Padre," she said. "I think she's gone."

And then she began to cry.

Padre Francisco held her for a long while and said nothing. I could tell he was melting on the inside. Not because of what she'd said but because of how often he'd heard things like that, how often he'd stood there and comforted those who had been left behind. Mami and Papi were blank and serious. Abuelo was quiet, and I watched as he stood two paces behind, studying us as if he knew what all this was about, had been there before in this church, by this altar, pleading to a priest about God snatching people out of other people's lives.

I felt a tug at my wrists. It was Pingüino.

"What?"

He pulled me away to the doors where Miguel leaned against the yellow hinges, staring at the sky. Pingüino beckoned to the table outside with the drinks, where Luis Rodríguez and the two strangers stood in a circle, deep in conversation. He tugged at Miguel's wrists. "Come on," he said.

"*¿Qué tú quieres, carajo?*" Miguel snapped.

"Let's go," Pingüino said.

"Why?" I said.

"Don't you want to know what they're saying?"

I tiptoed to see Luis through the chink of open door. I saw his brows drawn together and the gravity on the bearded men's faces. Whatever they were talking about, it looked serious.

"No," I lied.

"Seems like a stupid idea to me," Miguel said.

Pingüino rolled his eyes. "*Dios mío*, why can't you guys be fun for once? *Vámonos.*"

He led us into the daylight.

Outside the church, the lawn was balding, the ground brown from all the years of lunches in the sun. I'm not sure what most neighbourhoods did after church, but in Marianao people ate until their guts were as large as swallowed balloons. On the lawn, there were four long tables laden with food. The tables were really old— Padre Francisco said thirty years at least—and the edges had been worn down from bored children digging their utensils into the edges. On top of the tables were pots and pans of *arroz con pollo, picadillo, plátanos a puñetazos*, and sometimes if Doña Paula was in the mood, she would make ham *croquetas* Pingüino and I fought over.

There weren't *croquetas* today. There hadn't been any since Anita Valle had disappeared.

Everyone swarmed and made something resembling a line. They grabbed the creamy pink plates that belonged to the church and bunches of metal forks, spoons, and knives, which much like those of Doña Theresa, were speckled with age. Predictably, Tío Rodrigo had already made his first round and trudged by with a plate piled high with chicken legs, a serving of *picadillo* over that, and a massive heaping of *plátanos a puñetazos* on the side.

Near the stone path, Diego and Lucía fought over the rag doll. It had lost an arm, and now its shoulder was frayed with stuffing. He pushed her to the grass and she wailed. The grass stains on her butt were visible when she ran crying to her mother. Meanwhile, Luis and the strangers argued, Luis holding a forgotten glass of pineapple juice in his hand.

"Follow my lead and act casual," Pingüino said. "Don't ruin this, *tontos*."

"Pingüino," I said. "I don't think we should—"

"*Shhh*," he said. "*Cállate la boca*, and follow me."

Miguel rolled his eyes, but we followed Pingüino anyway, knowing deep down what a bad idea this was. Pingüino stood near Luis and the two strangers, and signalled for us to do the same. The three of us formed a loose semicircle with our backs to them.

Luis was speaking. "—can't believe you did something so stupid."

"Don't yell at us, we didn't know."

"You didn't tell us."

"I didn't tell you because I didn't know when—or if—you were coming back."

"So what do we do now?"

"I don't want to *do* anything."

"That wasn't part of the plan."

"I changed my mind."

"What? Why?"

"It doesn't matter."

"How can you say that? Of course it matters."

"Well—yes—but I don't want to—"

"We need to show them we don't knuckle under. We can't just do nothing."

"One more try. *Vámos*, Luis, just one more. We can do it the right way and then it'll be over."

"We'd be hurting people."

"Sometimes that's the price that must be paid."

"No, it isn't."

"They deserve it."

"No," Luis sounded desperate. "They don't."

"It was your idea. Isn't this what you wanted?"

"Yes, but I didn't want... I just want things back to normal."

One of them lowered his voice, and I leaned backwards to catch what he said. "Hey, Rodríguez, do you know those kids?"

A hand grabbed my shoulder gruffly. They grabbed Miguel and Pingüino too, and they turned us around. I realized they weren't men at all, but boys in their twenties, the same age as Luis. They hadn't washed their faces in a while and I could see the sheen of grime on their foreheads and cheeks. I could smell forest on their clothing and mud that stunk of rotten things. The man's hand tightened on my shoulder.

"What do you think, Luis?"

"I—I don't—"

Luis stopped. His eyes were fixed on something else. He perspired beneath his glasses. For once, he quit fidgeting.

Tío Rodrigo.

He sat at the corner of a table, his plate faint with streaks of sauce, his chair twisted in our direction. The green tablecloth fluttered at the corners. Tía Carmen sat next to him, and she rummaged in her bag for something, the wrinkles on her forehead worse than ever. Tío Rodrigo twisted something in his hands—a piece of grass, I think— except it had been destroyed by his fingers. Now, it was a mangled strand of something that might have once been alive, and he played with it mercilessly, his mouth in a thin line.

Luis and the strangers dispersed.

Miguel quivered beneath his father's stare.

13.
The Many Ugly Things

After church, it was the three of us on the front porch again.

"I saw the lights on in Rafi Consuelo's house," I said, as soon as Mami, Papi, and Abuelo went inside.

Pingüino's jaw dropped. "What?"

"This morning. Before the sun rose. Me and Mami saw the lights on."

"Are you sure?" Miguel asked. "It could've been another house."

"It was Rafi Consuelo's house. I know it."

"You're lying!" Pingüino said.

"I'm not."

"But…" Pingüino crossed his arms. "That's not fair."

"What?"

"I went there to throw away my letter and nothing happened. All Adela has to do is get up early and she gets to see all the action. Sometimes I think God doesn't like me."

"Don't make fun, Pingüino. This is serious."

"Are you *sure* it was his house?" Miguel asked again.

"*Yes*. Mami saw it too."

"Do you think he's back?" Pingüino said. He snuck a peek at Rafi Consuelo's house, as if he expected the lights to come blazing back on. "Maybe we should knock on the door. Just to see."

"*No!*"

"Why not?"

"We should tell Tío Rodrigo. What do you think Miguel?"

"No," Miguel said. "Definitely not. God knows what that would… No. You can't. You don't know…"

"What don't I know?"

Pingüino burst out all of a sudden, "Those rebels smelled bad, didn't they, Miguel?"

Miguel regained his composure, "Yes, they did."

"Pingüino, don't let Mami hear you saying things about rebels or she'll think I said something about the lights. She told me not to tell. Besides, you don't know they were rebels for sure."

"But they had beards like in the papers!"

"And if Don Manolo grew a beard, would that make him a rebel?"

"No… But Adela, they just were! And after that weird thing at Doña Theresa's house yesterday, you can't tell me Luis isn't a rebel too."

"What?" Miguel asked.

"We went over yesterday to pick lemons," I said, "and Luis came home while Doña Theresa was making lemonade. Things got strange."

So we told Miguel about the lemonade and Luis being awkward and saying sorry and Doña Theresa's lone figure in the hallway and how she had pulled herself off the ground and made us lemonade anyway.

"But what was he apologizing for?" Miguel asked.

The screen door whined open. Papi stood on the porch with his loafers shiny from this morning, sweat stains forming at the pits of his dress shirt.

"Pingüino, your mother wants you."

"*¿Qué?*"

"Your mother. She wants you."

"What for?"

"To clean the *basura* you left in your room," Mami said, emerging from the hallway, her apron on, faint notes of *guaracha* floating out from the kitchen. "I bet you thought me or Adela would clean it up, but oh no—Not in this lifetime, *señor*. Move your big Cuban butt. *Arranca*."

"*Pero* Mami—"

"Don't '*Pero* Mami' me. Clean your room. Now."

Pingüino faked a yawn and Papi smiled in amusement. Mami glared at Pingüino. "When I get there in ten minutes, I better see you working."

"Okay, okay. *Cálmate, Dios mío*." Pingüino trundled inside and Papi held the door for him.

"Adela, you should come inside too," Mami said, "I want to get Abuelo away from that television screen. I think he's going to go blind staring at that thing."

Miguel's face was gray.

"Can I have a few more minutes?" I asked.

"Maybe," Mami said. "How was the shoe shop the other day?"

"What?"

"When Papi picked you up from school and took you to the shoe shop."

I shrugged. "It was fine. We met Dulce's sister, Celia."

The floorboards creaked beneath Papi's feet.

"I didn't know Dulce had a sister. What's she like?"

I met Papi's eyes over Mami's shoulder. I couldn't tell if he was shaking his head, or if I was imagining it, if the sun was playing tricks on my eyes like on hot days when the heat made mirages of the sea and sky in Havana. I remembered Celia and her fuzzy top, the slit along her skirt, the cheap makeup. I remembered her face through the window as Papi steered her toward the sidewalk.

"She was nothing special," I said. "Why?"

"You might have to go to the shoe shop if I need to help Doña Theresa again."

"Oh… Can I stay outside then?"

"Only for a little bit. Carmen's been crazy ever since last week. She thinks if Miguel is out of her sight for more than a few minutes that the world will explode."

Miguel fidgeted and Mami didn't notice. She walked inside, the screen door rattling shut behind her. We stayed silent as we heard her rapid, one-after-the-other footsteps recede down the hall—city-goers' footsteps that, if you lay still enough, you could hear going late at night when she moved pots and pans around, cleaning up the kitchen. Papi went in after her. He shut the screen door without a sound.

In my head, I replayed everything that had happened. I thought about Tío Rodrigo in our living room saying there was nothing to be done. I thought about Sister Tula smacking María Viramontes for being different like José Martí. I thought about Mami kissing me on the forehead that morning, saying I must tell no one of the lights at the dead house. I thought about Papi shifting at the mention of Celia's name. I thought about Pingüino and his letter home, and the way Miguel had beat him up because Pingüino thought he was crying. I thought about Luis yelling at the two strangers and Doña Theresa sobbing in the hallway of her house with lemon juice dripping down her dress. I thought about Don Manolo's anger and Doña Paula's grief and the helplessness of it all. And it made my stomach feel too full, like it was filled to the brim with liquids and I was a water tower about to topple over because there were so many ugly things sifting around inside. I couldn't handle one more secret. I couldn't handle one more thing I couldn't talk about. Not one more drop.

"Adela," Miguel said, "Can I talk to you about something?"

14.

One More Drop

I lay in bed that night recalling Miguel leaning against the blue wall of our house as a lizard scrambled above his head. I remembered the tree at the side of the house we'd stood next to so Mami wouldn't hear us, and the shadow one of the leaves had made, a dim diagonal across his face.

There was something wrong with Tío Rodrigo. Miguel wouldn't tell me what it was, but it had to be bad because there had been droplets of sweat forming at the crown of his head as he said it and Miguel never sweat, not even when he played baseball in the summer. Miguel didn't know what was wrong with him. He was just different. Off. He'd been coming home late recently. He had always come home late every once in a while, but so far it had been almost every night that week. On some nights he refused to eat dinner. When he did, he ate little—only small servings of rice and beans and never any meat. The oddest thing was this: he couldn't stand the sound of bones breaking.

Miguel loved snapping the bones of his chicken and sucking out the marrow. On the few occasions over the last couple of weeks when Tío Rodrigo made it home on time for dinner, Miguel would crack the bones of the wing to slurp out the insides. And every time, Tío Rodrigo would wince and claim he needed to go to the bathroom. But a few nights ago, twenty minutes after dinner had come and gone, Miguel passed by the bathroom to get a glass of water, and he saw Tío Rodrigo's shadow under the doorway. When he moved closer, he heard laboured breathing. The panicky kind.

"There's something wrong with him," Miguel told me. "And I think there might be something wrong with me too."

"What do you mean?"

"Ever since last week, since—you know—the bombing, I can't walk on the street. I've done it a million times. I've walked from Marianao to the Hotel Nacional a million times in the dark past kids and women and men and drunks and maybe I got nervous, but I was never scared. Now it's like every time I see people reach for their pockets or stop to talk to someone, I think they're going to do something to me, I feel like I have to start running, and then all of a sudden I can't breathe and I have to stop at a corner and tell myself nothing's wrong, there's nothing to be worried about, that I need to get over it and get to work already. And I know it's dumb because I've done it a million times before and there's never been anything wrong. But it's different now. It's like there's something wrong with my head. Look, I know it's stupid and maybe I shouldn't be telling you this, it's just that… the way I breathe on my walk to work is what my dad sounded like on the other side of that door."

15

Rebelde

It had been another day of the shoe shop: warm gust of leather air, Dulce (this time, licking a cherry lollipop) with her feet up on the desk, the fan whining like its lungs were full of dust, the leather shoes sweating in the heat. And no Celia. A few customers strayed in and out, but none had her dark skin or her small waist or her clothes that were raggedy but pretty the way the feathers of dirty pigeons were, the ones in the alleyways of Old Havana that still had some gloss on them.

Every time the bell rang, Papi's eyes flicked towards the door and then back to whatever shoe he was shining at his desk, the powder creasing into the edges of his fingernails. And Dulce daydreamed at the ceiling, her lips colouring into the red of the lollipop. When it was time to go, we piled into Abuelo's car and Papi took a plain white shoebox and put it under the seat next to him.

By the time we got home, there was an orangey sherbert in the sky and the sun glowed a hot-iron red with no halo. Pingüino and I got out of the car and walked to the front door, leaving Papi behind in the front seat of Abuelo's car to smoke a cigarette. It wasn't uncommon for Abuelo or Mami or Papi to smoke a cigar on the front porch every once in a while, to see one of them blow smoke rings into the air, but cigarettes were different and I'd never seen Papi smoke one before. The smoke was something I wasn't used to. It was a white kind of acrid that lingered in the back of my throat long after I'd inhaled it.

When Pingüino and I opened the front door, Doña Paula and Mami were on the couch and they jumped in alarm. Scattered across the coffee table were papers with childlike handwriting. Doña Paula gathered them and pressed them to her chest. When she got up, she gazed at her doll shoes. I couldn't help noticing how small her feet were.

"I should go," Doña Paula said to the floor. "Thank you, Deianeira. God bless you."

"*Adiós*. Take care."

As Doña Paula swung open the screen door, Papi was on the other side, his hand about to grasp the handle. "Oh… *Buenos días*, Doña Paula."

"*Buenos días*, Don Sebastián."

Doña Paula scrambled out the door and down the stairs towards her house. Pingüino and I put our stuff down by the couch as Papi watched Doña Paula from behind the curtains. Mami was in the kitchen. She pulled out the big pan from the bottom drawer and a yellow-and-green tin can of olive oil from the pantry. I sat on one of the stools at the kitchen counter and Pingüino did too. Mami didn't reach for the radio. Papi made sure Doña Paula was out of sight before speaking.

"What was she doing here?"

Mami twisted the knob on the stove near the front, the one that hadn't got loose and popped off yet, the one that was rusting around the edges. "She wanted to speak with me."

"I thought it was Doña Theresa you were helping."

"I am helping her, but I'm helping Doña Paula too."

78

"With what?"

"I can't tell you."

"Why not?"

"Don't worry about it."

Papi stood over Mami. He was so close she must've felt his breath on her shoulder. She ignored him as she shifted the pots and pans around. Mami hefted the bag of white rice from the pantry and placed it on the counter.

"It better not be illegal," Papi said.

"Why would it be illegal?"

Papi ran his hands through his hair. "We've talked about this. We can't get any more involved with the Valles than normal."

"Sebastián, if you start again with one of your *rebelde* theories—"

"It doesn't matter what I think about the Valles. It matters what *they* think. The police are watching us. They're always watching us. Even Rodrigo is probably watching us. There's a rat somewhere in this town, I can smell it. If someone sees you with her, then what will they think? What if they think we're involved? What if we're next? What if the next person kidnapped in the middle of the night is you or me or worse—What if it's Pingüino or Adela? There is no one we can trust. We're alone."

"Why are you so hopeless? Why do you erase the good in everything?"

"Maybe you can't erase the good if it was never there in the first place."

"What?"

"I mean—I don't... I didn't mean to say that. What I'm trying to say, Deianeira, is that I can't control the world around us. No one can. The best any of us can do is survive."

"And what about living? What about that?"

"Survival comes first."

"You're unbelievable. Just because you're insecure doesn't mean the rest of us have to be."

"I never said that."

"No, but you're trying to make it that way. Do you ever think about what you do?"

"What?"

"Nothing. Never mind. I don't know why I try anymore."

Pingüino's bottom lip quivered. It was easy to forget sometimes he was only ten. I was reminded of that as his child hands were splayed on the counter in front of him, his fingernails like dainty Chiclets glowing in the dark.

"The meetings at this house are over," Papi said. "I forbid you to bring either Doña Paula or Doña Theresa here ever again. Is that clear?" Mami glared at him, and went back to the stove. Papi grabbed her by the shoulders and wrenched her towards him.

"Get your hands off me!" she screamed.

"Is that clear?" he said again.

Mami tried ripping herself from him, and they struggled a moment before he released her.

"*Imbécil*," she said, and I could taste the poison soaked into the words, could feel a sour aftertaste as the rest of them came out of her mouth. "I should have never married you."

And what hurt the most wasn't the poison or the anger or the hot-iron sun in the sky burning into oblivion. It wasn't Pingüino's child hands or Doña Paula's cramped doll shoes or Papi's cigarette smoke searing itself into the back of my throat. It was the tiredness creased into Papi's face, the sad wrinkles that sagged around the deadness in his eyes, the slow acceptance and indifference with which he absorbed Mami's words one by one and said absolutely nothing at all.

16.
The Night They Met

The night they met the whole city stopped glowing. That's how Papi always started it.

From afar, the city was a shell in the moonlight. Shining, white, ghostly. The buildings rising up. Ethereal. But on the streets it was different. The pavement hummed. *Guaracha* pounded the concrete, prostitutes lounged with their legs gleaming, cigar smoke drifted along the alleyways. And there was rum—a whole lot of it.

The boy was a mess. He was one of those country boys who'd never been to the city, the one who'd learned mambo from his grandmother in the parlour while his aunts stood around and made fun. The first time he rode in a car, he was twenty and it was the taxi from the train station to the University. He had a wisp for a moustache and doe eyes.

The girl was a queen with dark hair and even darker eyes. The first time he saw her smile, all there was was bright lipstick and the teensiest gap between her two front teeth. It was easy to imagine: a mint on her breath, red nail polish that smelled like alcohol, hips that swayed to the beat of the rhythm. The golden studs her mother gave her. Her neck sticky with sweat because she was the first one on the dance floor and the last to leave. He saw her and the streets stopped humming.

It used to be Papi would gather Pingüino and me on the couch in the living room, and tell the story in his loudest voice so Mami could hear it all the way in the kitchen, or the bedroom, or the hallway, or wherever she was in the house. Abuelo would grin in his big green armchair while Pingüino groaned and put a pillow over his head. And Mami would appear at the doorway with her arms crossed.

"*Y aquí está la muchacha hermosa*—Here is the beautiful girl!"

Inevitably, Mami—the girl who had grown up and become even *more* beautiful, Papi always said—would let out a giggle, and she would let Papi sweep her into his arms. He would have trouble picking her up because of the bottom of whatever dress she was wearing, would complain of the pain in his back ("*Pero Dios mío*, the boy has gotten old, hasn't he?"), and Abuelo, Pingüino, and I would laugh at their ridiculousness, at the mango-red blush creeping its way across Mami's face. They would kiss and all would be right with the world.

Papi hadn't told the story in ages.

The morning after Doña Paula and the papers, Papi was out on the porch smoking another cigarette. I woke up early and saw his outline pixelated by the mesh of the screen door. There was a mess of blankets and cushions on the floor of the living room. Papi had spent another night on the couch. He was wrapped in the thin blanket that smelled of mothballs. Next to him, a foggy glass was half-filled with rum that hadn't seen daylight since *Nochebuena* last year.

I opened the door and stood barefoot on the porch, the floor cool with early morning.

"Can I sit with you?"

A slow sad nod. The sound of a lizard scrabbling against the concrete.

I sat next to him, unwrapped part of the cover, and leaned into his chest. He smelled of rum and sleeplessness. He put a weak arm around me.

"*Ay, mi* Adelita. What are we going to do?"

I said nothing, and felt a faint fear that maybe I would have to. My stomach felt as if I was about to cry. Papi sighed and studied my hair.

"Your hair glows in the sunlight, did you know?"

I grabbed a strand and held it up to my eyes. "It looks dark to me."

"No, *mija*, not like that," Papi said, chuckling weakly. "It's along the edges. It turns golden in the sun."

"I guess."

The sun moved across the sky a few more inches before I dared to speak.

"Do you still love her?"

Papi was silent a good couple of moments before responding. I tried to see if I could find any of that boy in him, that ruggedness, that sweetness Mami had fallen for. I tried so hard, and refused to admit I had found nothing. I remembered the way he had grabbed her, and his arm around me felt heavy and dull. Papi took a sip from the foggy glass.

"Of course I do."

I got that crying feeling in my stomach again, and tried to ignore the heaviness inside me. I took hold of Papi's hand, and felt the country-boy calloused fingers that weren't glowing anymore, but were coloured the gray of cigarette ash drifting lost in still air.

"Tell me the story again, Papi."

He went quiet. So quiet, I could hear the wind moving between the leaves. Then, he began, in a voice as bittersweet as an old Cuban folk song.

"The night they met the whole city stopped glowing..."

As I listened, I watched the shadows move across the green of the lawn, the blue of the raggedy old house in Marianao where Mami and Papi had begun together, the front porch steps that had long since cracked in the heat. It felt like hours, but Papi and I were awake watching the world move together, huddled beneath the sunrise and a thin, mothball blanket.

17.

Las Noticias

Every day at around noon, Mami put on her dress that smelled of oldness, slipped on a pair of worn brown sandals, and checked the mail at the rotten clump of mailboxes in the overgrown jungle by the intersection. We didn't get much in the mail other than the odd letter from Tía Noelia, Papi's sister who lived on the plantation, and the money that Papi's uncle sent every few weeks. But on Friday, there was an extra bit of mail no one had been expecting, certainly not Pingüino. That day, Pingüino and I walked home from school, and as soon as we walked through the front door—

"What do you mean you put lizards in the teacher's desk?"

Pingüino froze. "What?"

From his armchair, Abuelo chuckled, and put down that day's newspaper to watch. "You're in for it now, *mijo.*"

"What?"

"Letter from your school today." Mami threw an envelope on the coffee table. The top of it had already been ripped open. "Read it."

Pingüino picked it up, and I read over his shoulder:

Dear Señora Santiago,

We write to inform you of conduct on the part of your son, Pedro Santiago, unbefitting of la Escuela Católica de la Virgen María. The conduct in question consisted of placing lizards in the desk of his *teacher, Sister Juana, severely scaring her and causing one student to faint... (*I skimmed on)*... This is Pedro's third offence, and in accordance with school policy we send this letter both with Pedro himself and in the mail. We hope this finds you well and that you will discuss the matter with Pedro in order to stop any further instances of incorrigible behaviour.*

Cordialmente,

Sister Moye

Directora de la Escuela Católica de la Virgen María

"Do you have anything to say for yourself?" Mami said.

"No. Except Sister Juana is a real screamer."

A ridiculous half-stifled laugh came out of Abuelo and me at the same time. Abuelo covered his mouth with his hand, and then slowly lifted his newspaper to cover his face. His forehead was bright pink beneath his hairline. Mami had that I'm-going-to-smack-you look on her face.

"The next time you talk back like that, *te voy a dar una galleta*. I'm going to hit you so hard you won't even know what year it is."

Pingüino swallowed a grin. "*Sí*, Mami."

"What did you do with the letter?"

The grin disappeared. "What letter?"

"The letter she sent home with you."

"I may have lost it."

"Don't talk shit *porque me tienes hasta el último pelo*. What did you do with it?"

"I threw it away."

Mami's nostrils flared. "You did *what*?"

Pingüino stayed silent.

"And *why* did you put lizards in the teacher's desk?"

"Because Sister Juana hates me!" Pingüino burst out. "She hates me because she knows English and thinks she's fancy and she's always telling me I'm stupid!"

"*Por Dios*, Pingüino!" Mami snapped. "Why can't you have some mercy on your mother? Do you think I like getting these letters? Do you think I like having to yell at you? I hate it. I hate that I have to talk to you like this, but you don't give me any choice. No one in this house gives me any choice. I can't even have some peace and quiet."

"Deianeira—" Abuelo said.

"All I ask is that you be good in school," Mami continued as if she hadn't heard, "and you can't even do that. I don't know how many times we've talked about this. Maybe you are just as stupid as Sister Juana says."

"*Pero...* Mami—"

"I don't want to hear it," Mami said. "You are grounded for three weeks starting today. No television, no baseball, no dessert, no going out during the weekends. And you're going to help me put the laundry up."

Pingüino didn't meet anyone's eyes. Mami moved to the kitchen and turned on the tap. Pingüino picked up his bag, and his lip quivered. He retreated into the hallway, the door of our room closing behind him. I sat carefully on the arm of Abuelo's chair hoping Mami wouldn't find a reason to pick on me too. She didn't. As the water ran, Abuelo flipped through the pages of his newspaper.

He sighed. "*Ya no puedo con las noticias*, I can't take the newspapers anymore."

"I don't know why you're surprised," Mami said, cleaning a plate with an old blue rag.

"You haven't even read it," I said.

"I don't have to. What is it? Someone got shot. Someone was arrested. Some rebels in the mountains. Batista says everything is fine. A lot of people were shot. A lot of people were arrested. The rebels are winning. The rebels aren't winning. Batista still says everything is fine. Everybody died. Is it ever anything different?"

"No," Abuelo said, "but they're still people."

Mami continued scrubbing. Even from the living room, I could see the plate she was cleaning was already spotless, could hear the grating of the fibres on ceramic, could see the pink rawness of her fingertips.

"Well, no one seems to remember that anymore."

Abuelo sighed. He folded the newspaper, and placed it on the floor by his feet. "Where's Sebastián?"

"At work. Where else?"

Abuelo glanced at me. "I heard the arguing the other day."

Mami stopped scrubbing. "You did?"

"I hear most things. I may be old, but I'm not deaf. Is everything—?"

"Everything is as it always is." Mami put the rag and the plate aside, "I think I'm going to take a nap. I have a headache."

She left the room and I listened as her footsteps faded down the hall. The door closed behind her too. Abuelo patted my hand. "Adela," he said, "Do me a favour and turn on the television for me. Let's see if there's anything worth watching, eh?"

18.
Ghost House

I couldn't sleep again that night. I was thinking too much. About Mami and Papi. About how after Mami had yelled at him, Pingüino hadn't talked to anyone for the rest of the day. About Anita Valle and how even though Miguel had told me not to, I couldn't stop imagining where she might be or whether she was alive or not. I got out of bed and when I did, Abuelo was in his room and Papi was on the couch so I decided to sit outside on the front porch.

Marianao was different in the dark. The stars were so bright it felt like someone had turned the lights on. The other houses were ghost houses, and I would've believed they were lifeless if it weren't for the cars parked out front and the other things that belonged to the people who lived there. Like Don Álvarez's banana cart resting in the garage and Don Manolo's ashtray a white speck in the distance. Even Rafi Consuelo's house had the broken fridge in the front yard, and if it weren't for the uncut grass maybe his house could've pretended to be alive too. But I knew better than that.

I looked and there was a figure in the road. It was Luis Rodríguez. He was sitting on the ground with his legs spread out in front of him. He was watching Rafi Consuelo's house. I waited for him to get up, but he didn't. Instead, he looked at the house and then laid down flat on his back as if to watch the stars, except it seemed like his eyes were closed and he covered his ears with his hands.

I remembered what Pingüino had said about him being a rebel, and began to panic. I tried to get up and tripped. "*Mierda*," I whispered, but it was still too loud.

He looked up and my stomach dropped. He stood and brushed himself off, embarrassed, before walking over.

"Oh… *Hola*, Adela."

"*Hola*, Luis."

We stared at one another.

"I didn't know you knew my name," I said.

"Of course. You were at my house."

"Picking lemons."

"Right, yes." Luis's eyes flickered. "Listen," he said, "I'm sorry for the other day. My mother can be a bit… Let's just say parents change when you get older."

"What?"

"Never mind, it doesn't matter."

His hands fidgeted, and I wondered if when he murdered me he would do it with his hands or pull a knife out from somewhere. I waited for him to speak, but he didn't.

"What were you doing out there?"

"Out where?"

"You were sitting in the street and then you laid down."

"I was—"

"Were you looking at Rafi Consuelo's house?"

"Why do you say that?"

"I don't know. It looked like you were looking at it. Everyone's always looking at it."

"I couldn't sleep. You?"

"I couldn't sleep either… Why were you lying in the middle of the road like that?"

"I'd tell you, but you'd think I'm crazy."

"Okay."

An awkward silence.

"I was listening to my own heartbeat."

"You were… what?"

"I know, it's strange," Luis said quickly, pushing up his glasses. "I just—sometimes I can't sleep because I get paranoid about things."

"What kinds of things?" I said, not really sure why I was asking. I could tell Luis was surprised I was asking him questions, and I was surprised too. But the moon was out and the air was nice and I didn't want to be inside anymore. I didn't want to see Papi sleeping on the couch or wonder why everything felt so wrong. I felt like knowing something for once.

"Just. Life things," Luis said. "Like if I'm doing things the right way. Or maybe that I'm fake for thinking I know what the right things are. Or maybe that I'm wasting time on the wrong things… Sorry, I know how strange that must sound."

"But I don't get it. Why were you listening to your own heartbeat?"

"Because sometimes when everything's too big, you need something small to concentrate on."

"Oh."

"Maybe you'll understand when you're older. How old are you again?"

"Thirteen."

"Really?"

"Yes. Why?"

"You seem older."

"What makes you say that?"

"I don't know. You seem older. Anyway, how is it?"

"What?"

"Being thirteen. I don't remember."

It was my turn to be surprised. I shrugged. "It's alright, I guess."

Luis smiled. "Really? Is that all you have to say? *No me digas.*"

"I don't know. It's a weird question. People don't normally ask me that."

"Well, I'm asking you now. How is being thirteen?"

"It's… hard. Probably easier than other things. But still hard."

"Why?"

"What do you mean 'why'?"

"Just… why?"

"I don't know. I don't know what I'm supposed to be doing, and…" I hesitated before saying it because it was something I'd never said out loud before, not even to myself, "Sometimes I feel like I'm dissolving."

I waited for him to stare at me strangely, but he didn't. He was looking at me like he was before, except maybe with a tinge of a smile on his face. I wasn't sure whether that made me feel better or if I wanted to smack him for it.

"Dissolving?"

"Yeah."

"Who makes you think that?"

"I don't think anyone makes me think that. I just do."

"Well, something must have made you think that way, Adela. You weren't born with those thoughts in your head."

"I don't—"

"Do you think it's because people aren't paying attention? To you, I mean."

"Maybe."

"Interesting."

"Why are you asking me these questions?"

"I don't know. We're out here because we can't sleep, we might as well make the most of it."

"Did you know Anita well? In school?"

"I wouldn't say I knew her well. But we know each other, yes."

"She was my babysitter. She was nice."

Luis nodded, and I imagined if I could see behind the glare of his glasses he would look sad. "I'm sure she was."

He was sad a moment longer. Then he spoke again.

"I think it's about time we went home," he said. "What do you think?"

"Sure. *Buenas noches*, Luis."

"*Buenas noches,* Adela. Oh—one more thing."

"Yes?"

"Maybe you should try listening to your own heartbeat sometime."

"…Okay."

"*Adiós.*"

He smiled and waved. I watched as he retreated to his house down the street, a silver body in the moonlight with a wrinkled shirt. When I got back to bed, I didn't think anything about Mami and Papi or Pingüino or Anita or Rafi's house. I sat under the covers and watched Pingüino's chest rising and falling. I tried listening to my own heartbeat. I couldn't hear it. So I sat there in the dark until I fell asleep, waiting for the small thing that might make the big things go away.

19

When the Rain Pours

It was Saturday and it was about to rain. The sky was white the way it was before a thunderstorm. It was fine because Pingüino was grounded and I didn't feel like walking over to Miguel's house anyway. I thought about telling Pingüino what had happened with Luis the night before, but that felt like something I wanted to keep to myself. At one point, Mami told us she was going to the grocery store, but other than that, the day had been uneventful. Now we were in our room staring at the ceiling.

"Adela?" Pingüino said, splayed out on his bed.

"What?" I said, splayed out on mine.

"I'm hungry."

"Then go get something to eat."

Pingüino rolled over onto his face. "No," he said into the pillow.

"Then why are you complaining?"

He rolled back over into a more regular position. "Because I'm hungry."

"I'm not going to get you something to eat."

"Why not?"

"You have legs, don't you?"

"You'd let your little brother starve?"

"In a heartbeat."

"You're horrible."

A long pause.

"Adela?"

"What?"

"Do you think Mami and Papi are going to break up?"

I wasn't sure how to reply. "I don't know," I said.

He sighed.

"Goddamn it," I said, getting up.

"What?"

"What do you want to eat?"

"*Ropa vieja,*" Pingüino said.

"Try again, *comemierda.*"

"Fine. Ham-and-cheese sandwich."

"Better."

I walked into the living room and Papi was pacing. There was a woman on the couch and I realized with a start the woman wasn't Mami. It was Celia. She wore lipstick and a skimpy red dress. "Oh, it's Adela," Celia said in a mild voice. "*Hola,* Adela."

Papi stopped pacing. He closed his eyes. "*Mierda,*" he whispered. He rubbed his face. "Adela. I thought you were in your room with Pingüino. Abuelo's still asleep, isn't he?"

"What is she doing here?"

"Go back to your room."

"You can't tell her what to do," Celia said.

"Sure, I can. She's my daughter."

"She's a person," she said to Papi. "You're a person," she told me as if I didn't already know, "You do what you want to do."

I regarded her skimpy red dress and her makeup, which was the same as the last time I had seen her at the shoe shop. "She's a whore, isn't she?" I asked Papi.

"You don't have to be so rude about it," Celia said, checking her nails.

"What?" Papi said.

"She's a whore. Just like the girl you screamed at."

"What girl?" Papi said.

"You don't remember? You were laughing with Pingüino about something and there was a prostitute standing at the curb and you called her a *puta* through the window."

"What does that have to do with anything?"

"Everything!" Celia said, standing up. "It's a lack of *love* is what it is."

"*Shhh*," Papi said, "Do you want the whole house to hear?"

"Is she crazy or something?" I said.

"Why can't you tell me?" Celia said.

"Why do you need to know?" Papi said.

"Because it's not enough."

Papi glanced at me. "Not here."

"For God's sake, Sebastián. Your kids saw me at the shoe shop and now I'm in your house. I know that Adela, for one, isn't stupid."

"Mami's going to be home soon," I said.

"See? She's already figured it out. Go on, Adela. Tell your father what you know."

"What?"

"You're a smart girl. You already know what I am, tell him what else you know."

I didn't know if I wanted to say it out loud. There would be no pretending after this.

"You're having an affair," I said.

Papi stopped pacing and looked at me.

Celia beamed. "There you go," she said.

Papi threw his hands in the air. "Has the whole world gone mad?"

"Yes. Isn't it wonderful?"

"What is wrong with you?"

"I love you. I've never been in love before."

"Stop saying that."

"Why can't you tell me you love me too?"

"I'm married."

"That hasn't stopped you before."

"I never said I loved you."

"I just want to know, Sebastián, please?"

Papi sighed and sat on the couch, rubbing his temples.

"You know, Mami is going to be home soon and—Where are you going?"

Papi got up and walked outside. I looked at Celia and she shrugged. I went to the window and watched as he ripped open the door of Abuelo's car to rummage around beneath the seats. He came out of the car with a white box in his hands. It was the box from the shoe shop. The sky became a dark, violent gray, and the rain poured. The raindrops struck the hood of Abuelo's car so hard it sounded as if it were being bludgeoned with marbles. The road in front of our house turned into a rippling river, the rain making the surface dance. Papi stood with the white box in the downpour, his clothes soaked, his bare feet in the mud. His hair was plastered. Through the window our eyes met.

"Wait, what's she doing here?" Pingüino walked out from the hall and eyed Celia as she stood in the corner.

"It's complicated, *mijo*," she said, and lit a cigarette. It filled the air with a white acrid scent.

"You can't smoke in here," Pingüino said.

"Why not?"

"I don't know," he said. "You just can't."

"Those are the same cigarettes Papi was smoking the other day," I said.

"Hmmm," Celia said. She took a drag and blew out the smoke, "Wonder who got him hooked."

Papi came back in and shoved the soaking white box into Celia's hands. "Here you go. If that doesn't tell you what you need to know, I don't know what will."

She took off the top, and there was a crackling of tissue paper. "Oh," she said. "They're beautiful." She picked up one of the red shoes from the inside and I recognized them as the tattered flamenco shoes she'd fallen in love with on that day in the shoe shop.

"I was going to clean them and make them new, but you didn't give me the chance."

"Who is she?" Pingüino said.

"Papi's girlfriend."

Pingüino blinked, "What?"

The front door crashed open. Mami stood in the doorway with two giant wet paper bags full of groceries. They were slipping out of her hands. "Adela," she said, "Help me please, they're falling."

I rushed forward to grab the bags by the bottom, but it was too late. The cans of olive oil, the tomatoes, the bag of rice, the milk carton, the red peppers, the chicken, the onions, the garlic, the black beans, the bread, the cheese, the eggs—all of it came tumbling out onto the floor. The eggs cracked and the milk spilled. The tomatoes rolled across the floor.

"*¡COÑO!*" Mami screamed.

"*¿Qué carajo está pasando?*" Abuelo said, emerging from his room. "Can't a man sleep in peace?"

Mami noticed Celia for the first time. "Who are you?"

"Papi's girlfriend," Pingüino said, "Apparently."

I wanted to strangle him, but mostly I wanted to strangle Papi.

"She's his what?" Abuelo said.

"Celia, get out of here," Papi said.

"But I—"

"NOW!"

Mami picked up one of the cans of olive oil off the floor and threw it at Papi. "I KNEW IT! YOU BASTARD!"

"Celia, get out of here!"

Celia did as she was told. She shoved her red shoes back into the box and disappeared into the rain.

"*¿ESA PUTA?* THAT'S WHO YOU'RE SLEEPING WITH?"

"Deianeira, *por favor, cálmate—*"

"HOW *DARE* YOU TELL ME TO CALM DOWN?"

She picked up another can of olive oil and chucked it at his head. He ducked just in time. She stormed over and kicked him, slapped him, raked him with her nails. And he didn't even fight back. He curled into himself and took it. She scratched his cheek and it began to bleed. It took a few seconds for Abuelo to intervene and pull her off of him. She crumpled to the floor, sobbing. But it was all over her—the blood. Papi's blood. I never thought a cut on the cheek would bleed so much. The scent of it mingled with Celia's cigarette smoke. Abuelo got on the floor and rocked her like she was a little kid saying, "Shhh, shhh."

Papi wiped the blood on his pants even though he was wet. His fingers were covered in red, running into the lines of his handprints.

He saw us, standing by the couch. It was then that I realized I had wrapped my arms around Pingüino, that I was holding his head against my chest so he wouldn't have to see. He had begun to cry and his mucus and saliva soaked into my shirt.

"Go to your room," Papi said.

"Come on," I whispered to Pingüino. "Come on, let's go."

He wouldn't move. Mami yowled while Abuelo wiped her face with his shirtfront and murmured things to her. Papi went into the kitchen and cleaned his cheek with one of the towels Mami kept by the oven.

"*Vámonos*," I said to Pingüino. I unwrapped myself from him, and guided him towards the room, his nose running. There was a loose blanket on the floor—the same thin, dusty one Papi and I had wrapped around ourselves as we sat beneath the sunrise—and Pingüino stumbled over its mangled form like it was road kill. In our room, he collapsed onto his bed facedown, paralysed, with a muffled scream of "*¿Por qué, por qué, por qué?*" And because I could not answer, I sat next to him and stroked his feathery hair that resembled Papi's as I told myself I would not cry though my insides felt dead. In the room next door, voices murmured. When I went to the window, the neighbourhood lights were on.

20.
Papi and Celia

Papi met Celia by accident in December before Christmastime. It was Jorge Luciano's bachelor party, and Papi said he couldn't say no, that Jorge had been one of his only friends from college who'd come from the same dirt he had way out in the countryside, that they'd grown up a few miles away from each other, which in those parts was like living right next door. He'd told him he didn't want to go to a brothel, but Jorge wouldn't listen and so he'd been dragged along in a car full of *borrachos*, drunk on cheap rum with stains all down their fronts. Celia was the prostitute they'd given him, and he swore he hadn't slept with her that first time. It was just talking about dumb things like his job at the shoe shop and his kids and the rebellion and how damn bored he'd been lately going in an endless cycle from home to work and back again, about his family in Marianao and how useless he felt in the Zapatería de Cuba in Old Havana where the same customers filed in and out and Dulce sat bored at her desk… That's how they had found out the funny coincidence; Celia was Dulce's sister. So they got to talking in the alleyway outside the brothel, smoking cigarettes while Jorge Luciano and the boys disappeared to God-knows-where. The whole city was dressed up for Christmas, the signs all down the street looped up in golden garlands, yellow stars, copper bells—even the furniture stores and the barber shops were decked out.

That was how it began. Everything after that was just details. Celia would loiter outside the shoe shop on certain afternoons, bright ones when the toothless man on the corner sold bags of oranges to stopped cars on the intersections, gloomy ones when the flags outside people's shops fluttered harshly in the wind. It became so that those days Celia showed up outside the doorstep were sacred days, like finding a peso lodged in the cracks of the cobblestone. She was a radiant indulgence, one Papi had no plans of falling in love with.

The first and last time Papi slept with Celia was on a Wednesday. The same day as the bombing at the Hotel Nacional. It was at her place, a tiny box-shaped apartment in the ghettoes where the buildings were tangled in laundry lines heavy with clothing. The place itself was only a few years old, but the poverty of its residents had worn it down until it was as sad as Celia's sagging old mattress. He told Mami that after they were finished, as he dressed himself to leave, he looked out the window, saw the glowing white facade of Havana in the distance, and broke down as he was reminded of Mami and how in love he'd been the night he first saw her. He resolved he would never see Celia again, no matter how radiant her smile was, no matter how much he needed a break from the monotony of home and work and Marianao and the rusted bell that barely ever rang in the Zapatería. He told Celia too, that very night. But she hadn't believed him. You'll come back for me, she'd told him in the squalor of her apartment. You always do.

Except she'd come for him over and over again. The whole thing was a mistake, Papi knew that now. He should have never done it.

"So you never loved her?" Mami asked, at the end.

It was night now and the rain had died down to a cloud of dampness hanging over the street. Pingüino had fallen asleep in his bed, in the same position he had first collapsed, the tears dried onto his cheeks. Mami and Papi were in the living room with a single lamp on. I was curled up in the hallway, listening. I'd been there so long I felt my bones were going to meld into the wall, that I would be fossilized there forever. Papi's voice was parched for forgiveness.

"No," he said.

"Why are you here?"

"Because I love you. I know that now."

"You weren't sure?"

"Deianeira, *por favor*…"

"I gave up everything when I married you."

"I know."

"I gave you thirteen years of my life when I could have been anything."

"I know—I know that. I'm sorry."

"Sorry? Is that all you have?"

"Are you going to kick me out?"

"You don't seem sorry."

"I am, I promise you, I am."

"Tell me the truth this time."

"About what?"

"Do you love her?"

"It's not like that."

"What's it like then?"

"I don't know. But it's not as straightforward as either of us would like it to be."

"Then why did you do it?"

"I told you. I felt—trapped."

"By what?"

"Everything."

"You're lying."

"I'm not."

"I don't know how long I can keep doing this."

"Maybe we're both trapped."

"That's not an excuse."

"Deianeira?"

"What?"

"Do you remember what I said about survival?"

"That it comes before living?"

"Yes."

"What about it?"

"It was survival."

"Why do you get to survive and I don't?"

"What?"

"You don't know anything, do you?"

"I guess not. Are you going to kick me out?"

"No. Not tonight."

A dim light flooded the hall. I thought Abuelo had retreated to his room, but now he stood over me without his glasses.

"*Vámonos, mi* Adelita," he told me. He talked in barely a whisper. He took my hand and helped me up. "I think it's time to go to bed."

He did the same thing Papi used to do when we were little. He carried me to my room, put me in my bed, and pulled the covers up to my chest. Then he kissed me on the forehead, and said, "*Buenas noches*, Delita." He closed the door, and I watched until the light beneath my door faded away. As soon as it was gone, I fell into a troubled sleep.

21.
Apologies

The house was quiet. Pingüino was asleep in his bed, Papi was passed out on the couch with a blanket, and nothing stirred behind Abuelo's closed door. If a stranger had seen our living room that morning, they would have found nothing amiss; the twirling dust mites of the air, the couches so still it was as if they wanted to talk, the kitchen spotless, all the occupants of a perfect blue house dozing peacefully. But there were small things. Bits of eggshell on the floor. Dents in the wall from the cans of olive oil. Papi's shapeless form beneath the covers. Half-wet streaks of blood and rainwater. Most of the evidence had been swept away, but not all of it. I went to Mami's room and found the door half-cracked. I pushed it open.

Inside there was nothing but a pile of empty sheets. Her black church heels were missing from the closet and so was one of her nice dresses, a lilac one she'd bought a few years ago from somebody's sister. I told myself she'd probably gone to church for some alone time and that was it, but I wasn't so sure. It was unlike her. Then again, most of what had been going on was unlike her. Mami had never cried before. Maybe she had come close, but I had never seen any tears fall. Not once. Not even a few years ago when a friend from college, Lourdes, was killed accidentally when she walked into a shootout between the police and a couple of kids trying to rob a jewellery store. In the end nothing was stolen, the windows of the jewellery store were obliterated, the policemen were unharmed, one of the robbers suffered from a broken pinky, and Lourdes was facedown in a puddle of blood at the centre of the street, a shopping bag in her hand and inside a new satin bullet-bra and some underwear. When Mami heard, she was wordless for a few days. Later, she left to visit Lourdes's parents in Cerro and after she came back, it was as if nothing had happened. Everything was normal again. I didn't know how things would go from here on out.

I was light-footed when I went to the kitchen. I tried not to wake Papi whose snoring drifted through the air. In the sink, I saw two dirty glasses and a pair of spoons with speckles along the edges. They were from Doña Theresa's house, from that day with the lemonade and Luis and Doña Theresa sobbing in the hallway.

Without thinking, I grabbed the glasses and spoons, slipped on some sandals from my room, and stumbled out of the house in my nightgown. I walked the two houses down to Doña Theresa's house and banged on the door. I didn't expect anyone to be there, but I felt like pounding on somebody's door. It was Sunday morning and most of Marianao was deserted, the people packed into sweaty pews at church with the doors open. Which was why I almost fell over when Doña Theresa's door swung open, and behind it was Luis, a fresh bruise blooming across his cheek. The middle of it was eggplant-purple and the rest of his face was in shadow.

"Oh… *Hola*, Luis."

"*Hola*, Adela," Luis said, smiling.

I waited for him to invite me inside or take the glasses and spoons from my hands or maybe tell me something about my heartbeat again, but he just stood there smiling, which must have hurt with the bruise on his cheek. I cleared my throat, "I forgot to wash the glasses over at my house. Do you mind if I wash them in your sink?"

"Sure you can. I'm not doing anything important anyway."

It was only after I was across the threshold that I realized a series of unfortunate facts: (1) I was alone with Luis Rodríguez in an empty house; (2) I was dressed only in my nightgown and sandals; (3) no one knew where I was; (4) there was probably a reason why Doña Theresa had chosen to leave Luis at home rather than take him to church; and (5) almost every home within the immediate vicinity was deserted with the exception of my house whose occupants were asleep. On the other hand, Luis was acting somewhat normal today, and he hadn't done anything terrible to me the last time I'd seen him. Besides, it was too late to change my mind. I was already in.

As I moved into Doña Theresa's kitchen, the familiar sights greeted me. The blue-and-white wallpaper peeling near the ceiling, and the sink lined with rust, and the big windows in the back with the lemon tree brambles peering over the bottom edge. I put the glasses and the spoons on the counter. Luis installed himself in a seat in the corner. Now that his face was in the light, I could see a nasty gash on his forehead that had already scabbed over.

"How's school?" Luis asked.

"Fine."

"What are you learning about?"

"José Martí."

"Oh, good. I love José Martí."

"I don't know why people like him so much."

"He's the classic hero, I guess."

"Not really. He got shot. That's not very heroic."

"You're right," Luis said, laughing. "That's not heroic at all."

I'd never heard him laugh before, and he had a nice laugh. It was airy and carefree. "You agree with me?" I said.

"Yes, I suppose I do," he said, amused. "But I think it's better that way. It makes him different."

"But why do you love him so much?"

"He was a very hopeful man. Have you ever heard of—?"

"*Cultivo una rosa blanca?*" I said, finishing his sentence.

"Yes. Are they teaching that in school now?"

"No. It's my father's favourite poem."

"Must be a good man then."

I stayed silent.

"Did he tell you the origin story?"

"No."

"Rumour has it José Martí wrote the poem in jail after a friend turned him in to Spanish authorities."

"Not a very good friend then."

"No, he wasn't. But Martí forgave him anyway. If you choose to see it that way."

"What other way is there to see it?"

Luis shrugged. "It's poetry. Count the number of people on the planet and then multiply it by infinity. That's how many meanings a poem can have."

"He couldn't have just forgiven him like that, could he?"

"I suppose it could have been a form of defiance. He did send it to him afterwards."

"If my friend did something like that to me, I'd probably want to kill him."

"I think that may have been the point."

"To kill him?"

"No," Luis said. I waited for him to explain, but he didn't.

I went over to the sink and began washing the glasses and spoons with a pink rag I found at the bottom along with a few bloated grains of rice. When I reached for the soap, I saw there was a towel with some blood on it, though not as much as the one Papi had used last night. I figured it was for the gash on Luis's forehead, and I pretended not to see it as the water from the faucet came out with violent force, splattering against the metal bottom of the sink.

"What happened to your face?" I said.

"I fell."

"Oh," I said, not believing him. "My dad fell too, just yesterday. He cut open his cheek and there was so much blood, like you wouldn't believe. It got all over the floor, and I think my mother forgot to clean it up, so it's still there. It's eerie walking by a puddle of blood, even when you know the reason it's there isn't that big a deal…"

I was finished with the first glass and I moved on to the second, my sleeves turning transparent from the water.

"You know, my brother would have been here, but he got punished. He put lizards in the teacher's desk and then ripped up the letter the principal sent home."

"Your brother couldn't come?"

I was finished with the second glass, and now I was on to the spoons, scrubbing over the rough spots of rust on the handles. "No."

"Does he know you're here?"

I felt self-conscious in my nightgown all of a sudden. I had the uncomfortable feeling that Luis's eyes were boring into my back where my bra would be if I had to wear one, that he was trying to stare straight through my nightgown. A wisp of hair fell in front of my face and I blew it away because my hands were wet. I considered lying, but something told me if I lied, Luis would see right through me.

"No."

I jumped as Luis's chair rasped against the floor. The ceiling was high so the sound echoed and grated. An army of goosebumps sprouted on my arms. Luis was leaning across the countertop, his hair stringy and greasy and drooping over, his bruise brighter in the light.

"Can I tell you something?"

I was very aware of the spoon still in my hand, the soapsuds still slippery on my fingers.

"I lied," he said, and his voice went soft. "I didn't fall. It was those two men you saw at church."

I wanted to put down the spoon and turn off the water that was pummelling the sink and whining through the faucet. But if I moved, something in the air would break. He would stop, and I would never know about the two strangers.

"Who are they?"

"Who are they?" Luis laughed, and this time it didn't sound nice at all. "It doesn't matter who they are. But you understand, Adela, don't you? You know about lying too. We're liars, the both of us."

"I don't know what you're talking about."

"Your father did not fall."

Something got caught in my throat. "What?"

"Your father," Luis said, emphasizing each word, "did not fall. I saw it, Adela. A woman in a skimpy red dress goes in. Your mother goes in after her. The skimpy woman leaves. The screaming travels through the night. It's not hard to figure out what happens next."

"Why are you doing this?"

"Do you love your father?"

"What?"

"Do you love your father?"

I stared at him.

"It's a hell of a hard road to forgiveness."

I rinsed my hands beneath the running water. My eyes were tearing up, but I didn't want Luis to see. So I turned off the water with some effort (even the handle was rusted), and gazed at the corner where the wall met the ceiling, where the wallpaper was peeling and revealed an ugly brown stain.

"Please forgive me," Luis said. He sounded as if he was about to cry.

I wondered if I should walk over and comfort him, but I shuddered at the thought of putting my hand on his shoulder. Instead, I left the glasses and the spoons in the sink with the bloated grains of rice, and I walked around the countertop and sat at the stool next to him, the same stool I had sat in the week before as Doña Theresa had squeezed lemons into the juicer.

"Forgive you for what?"

Luis took off his glasses and cleaned them on his shirt. Without them, his head was like a gigantic cantaloupe with pushpins for eyes, and when he put them back on, his glasses were even foggier than before.

"Do you like President Batista, Adela?"

"I—I don't—"

Luis leapt from his chair and grabbed my shoulders, "Don't you see? How everyone is too scared to say it? And if they don't say it, nothing gets done. I *did* something, Adela."

"What did you do?"

He let me go and I gripped the counter. And as I sat there, I think he saw me clearly for the first time, saw the fear that must have been scrawled across my face, heard the words coming out of his mouth, and realized what they must have sounded like.

"I did the right thing," he said, "I swear."

I didn't care about being polite anymore. I didn't care that Luis was a sad, pitiful twenty-year-old who could go from discussing José Martí one moment to throttling thirteen-year-old girls the next. I didn't care about Doña Theresa or her glasses and spoons I had abandoned in the sink next to the bloated rice grains and Luis's bloodied towel. I wanted to get out of that house, and I never wanted to set foot in it ever again.

And so, I left Luis sobbing against the countertop with his greasy drooping hair, and his tearstained glasses, and his eggplant-purple bruise. I walked out of the door past Doña Theresa's pristine white rocking chair and her cream-coloured walls. And when I saw Doña Theresa on the street in Marianao on the way back from church with her hair rolled up and her soul-filled eyes, she waved, her bag draped over her arm. But I didn't wave back. Instead, I sprinted up the concrete stairs of my small blue house and slammed the screen door behind me, never once thinking of going back.

22.
The Arrest

The two strangers were arrested a week and a half later. It was a hot afternoon on a weekday and Pingüino and Mami were pinning up damp laundry on the lines in the front yard, which hung from the metal posts where the hammock used to be (Miguel and Pingüino broke it a few years ago when they both tried to get into it at the same time and the strings snapped). It had been a week and a half of Sister Tula teaching algebra and a chalkboard filled with Xs and Ys, of Miguel and I riding our bikes around Marianao feeding stray dogs while Pingüino stayed home and sulked, of Abuelo shaking his head every time he saw the news in *The Havana Post*, of Papi exiled to the couch at night ("My neck hurts *con cojones*," he said every time he rose with rat-nested hair in the mornings), of Mami slamming doors whenever Papi tried talking to her or woke up early to buy Mami's favourite breakfast from the Panadería two streets over: *pastelitos de guayaba*.

Pingüino had to do the job I normally did, and I watched, gloating, from the bottom step.

"How's it going, *hermanito*?" I said.

"Shut up," he told me.

"*Oye*," Mami said, "*Cállense los dos*."

"*Pero* Mami, this is a sissy job."

"No, it's not. *Ahora cállate, mijo*."

Pingüino glared as he held the bowl of clothes pegs—a mixture of wooden, metal, and plastic ones, all of them a collection from years of Mami thinking she'd lost some, buying more, and then finding them again. Mami stood on a wobbly chair with one leg shorter than the others. She had to stretch a little bit to pin the wet dresses, the pants, the shirts, the bras, the underwear. At the moment it happened, Mami was pinning up my stuffed bunny with the pink ribbon on it Tía Carmen had given me as a baby. She'd washed it because as she went around picking up discarded clothing from the floor of our room, she saw Rubia (that was its name) and realized it was three shades darker than it was supposed to be from years of me drooling on it as I slept.

She had just clipped it up by the second ear, when we heard a scream from down the street in the direction of Doña Theresa's house. Mami almost fell from her chair, but she steadied herself by grabbing Pingüino's shoulder and digging her nails in.

"¡Ay!" He dropped the bowl on the floor, and the clothes pegs went everywhere.

"Sorry, Pingüino," Mami said, letting go. She stepped down, steadying herself on one of the posts. She peered down the street. "¿Pero, coño, qué pasa?"

The answer came soon after. The two strangers looked different. Now they were clean-shaven. They had gotten new shirts that were white and crisp like the just-washed linen I imagined was put on the beds of the Hotel Nacional every morning. They were running and there were sweat stains on their shirts. As they came closer, I saw that their eyes were red-rimmed and bulging.

Behind them was Tío Rodrigo. The last time I had seen him was two weeks ago at church when he watched Luis and the strangers on the lawn. In that time, he had become a stickman skinnier than even Miguel. The outline of his ribs was creased into his shirt, his shoulders had lost their broadness, and he seemed shrunken in his police uniform. His head was skeleton-like beneath his policeman's cap, the brown of his skin drawn taut over the hollows of his eyes and cheeks. A few feet behind him was Tío Rodrigo's partner, Manuel, a heavyset man with a thin moustache tickling his upper lip.

Tío Rodrigo was gaining on them. All around us, faces appeared at windows, and doors whined open. Don Manolo came out onto his porch and squinted at the approaching figures. Doña Theresa did the same, clutching at the white rocking chair with one hand and at her heart with the other. Down the street, Doña Paula's face appeared at the window, Diego peeking around the curtain next to her.

Tío Rodrigo caught one of them right before they got to Rafi Consuelo's house. He tackled him and they both went sprawling onto the asphalt. Tío Rodrigo climbed on the man's back with the handcuffs and the man let out a guttural scream. Mami gasped. Pingüino flinched. Doña Paula swept the curtain across the window. Doña Theresa put her hands over her mouth. Don Manolo stumbled back inside.

"Manuel! *¡Agárralo!* He's getting away!" Tío Rodrigo said.

Manuel wheezed as he tackled the second man on Rafi Consuelo's uncut lawn near the abandoned refrigerator. He cuffed him and the man spat blood and blades of grass from his mouth. Over on the asphalt, Tío Rodrigo was having issues restraining the first man. Mami stepped onto the sidewalk as if to help.

"Deianeira, stay over there… Where is the goddamn car?"

A black-and-white police car came squealing down the street and burnt rubber tore the air apart. The one with the grass in his mouth went quietly as Manuel shoved him in headfirst. His lips were smeared in blood and I could tell he thought that wherever this car was taking him, he was going to die there. Once in, he observed his lap as if he hadn't noticed it before.

The second man fought like hell. I recognized him as the one who had grabbed me at church, and now that he was in front of our house I could see that his knuckles were bruised from punching Luis in the face. The man bit Tío Rodrigo in the arm, and Tío Rodrigo pulled out his police baton. He pushed the man onto the hood of the car. He brought the baton down on the man's arm. A sickening crack. A scream red with pain. The man's wrist broke, and his hand flopped onto the hood of the car. I wanted to throw up.

Tío Rodrigo straightened his policeman's cap, embarrassed, as if he'd been caught with his zipper down. After saying something to Manuel, he got into the car and they drove away without a siren or a single flashing light.

My stuffed bunny had been the last item to be clipped up. I watched it hang from the line by its ears, swinging in the air with dark button-eyes as Mami, Pingüino, and I began to pick up the clothes pegs from the porch and the grass. Over on Doña Theresa's porch, the rocking chair still rocked, its emptiness wanting someone to touch it lightly, to make it all end.

23.
For the Cruel One

Night had fallen and Pingüino and I were spread out in front of the television on our bellies, the carpet leaving imprints on our elbows. We were playing dominoes. Abuelo sat in his green chair watching television, and Mami was in the chair across from him flipping pages of an old book with great care. Papi was cooped up in his room listening to the radio as he had been for the past few days because no one wanted to talk to him. He rarely left except when Mami went into the room to go to sleep, and when he was in the room during the daytime, he would wait for someone to walk by so he could talk to himself or cheer at a baseball game—and I wondered how long he could stand living that way, waiting for people to notice he was alive.

"I've only got one left, Adela," Pingüino said. "Are you sure you don't want to give up?"

"I could still lock the game."

"And Miguel could get a girlfriend."

"You're mean."

"What? I'm just telling the truth."

I studied my dominoes, knowing I couldn't win. Abuelo tore his eyes away from the television, and leaned over my shoulder, studying my pieces with his tongue out.

"She can't lock me out, can she?" Pingüino asked.

Abuelo's face remained blank. "I have no idea."

"Whatever he says, don't listen to him," Mami said without looking up. "He's a horrible cheater."

"I am not," Abuelo said. He leaned closer and whispered, "She's just upset because I always win."

Mami rolled her eyes, half-smiling. She closed the book and laid it on her lap.

"Mami, what are you reading?" I asked.

"My diary from college. I found it in my closet. It has everything. The first day of school, the first time I met my friend Lourdes, the first time I met your father..."

Abuelo drummed his fingers on the arm of his chair. Pingüino poked me in the shoulder.

"Quit stalling, Adela. Do you have anything or not?"

"I—"

Papi's door creaked open and he walked past the living room into the kitchen without so much as glancing at us. We avoided looking at him. He went to the fridge and opened it. He got out the plastic gallon of Abuelo's coconut water and poured it in a glass before sitting in the centre of the couch, alone.

"Do you mind if I have some?" Papi said to Abuelo.

Abuelo shook his head with his eyes at his lap, "No, not at all."

There was a knocking on the door, a beating of fists, and it startled us. Papi got up to answer and his glass of coconut water spilled onto the floor. When he opened the door, Celia collapsed through it.

"Celia?" I said.

"*Ay Dios*, here we go again," Abuelo said.

Celia was on her knees and she was shaking. She wore the same outfit she had worn that day at the shoe shop—the fuzzy off-the-shoulder top, and the skirt with the slit in it, and the high heels. Her top was ripped at the shoulder and it flapped like a piece of half-peeled skin. Her teeth were smothered thickly in blood. There was a bruise forming on her cheek, and another on her neck, and another on her arm. Another one lidded Celia's left eye shut like a rotten grape.

"Help me, for God's sake."

Papi yanked her up by the arm and shook her.

"I told you not to come back here!" he screamed.

"Don't touch her that way," Mami snapped. "Can't you see she's hurt?"

Papi let go and Celia fell to the floor crying.

"This wasn't supposed to happen, this was never supposed to happen," Celia sobbed.

"Adela, help her to the couch please," Mami said. She was already in the kitchen, wetting a rag.

"What? Are you serious?" Pingüino asked.

"Yes, I'm serious."

I hesitated before touching her because I didn't know how to grab her, and I didn't know where to touch her so it wouldn't hurt. When I did, her skin was warm, but she pulled away and staggered to her feet. She sat in the middle of the couch where Papi had been.

"What happened?" Papi asked, nearing her.

"I'm sorry, I couldn't think of anywhere else," Celia said, and she latched onto him. "I'm sorry, I'm so sorry…"

"Celia—"

"I told him—I told him I didn't want to and he just—*Ay Dios, Jesús, Santa María, perdónenme*—"

"Here," Mami said, handing her the wet rag. Celia held it to her face and a strand of bloodstained saliva dribbled down her chin.

"Dulce told me, she told me it would happen if I stayed because it always happens but I never thought—I thought I could handle it—I didn't think it would happen like that—"

"Celia," Papi said, "What *happened*?"

"He…" Celia gulped, her eyes darting to where Pingüino and I were huddled. I was aware of the scent of coconut juice in the air, of the anger building in Papi's eyes, of Pingüino's trembling lips, of the glare of Abuelo's glasses, of the faint resentment in the way Mami regarded Celia's wine-dark skin. "He raped me."

Pingüino's forehead crinkled and I could tell he didn't know what the word meant. I dreaded to think how things would change when he did. Papi's face was smooth and still.

"Who did it?" Papi said.

"There's nothing you can do."

"Where is he?"

"He'll kill you."

"I don't care."

"Yes, you do. He'll kill anyone who ever mattered to you."

"Who is he?"

"I'm not telling you."

"Is he one of your clients?"

"Yes."

"You tried to quit didn't you?"

"Yes."

"It's my fault."

"No, it's not."

"Did you want to quit because of me?"

"Yes."

121

"Then it's my fault."

"There's nothing you could have done."

"There's plenty I could have done," Papi said, and he met Mami's eyes over Celia's shoulder. He refocused on Celia's face. "I can do something now."

"You can't."

Papi snarled and grabbed her wrist. Celia yelped and her hand turned a dead ash-grey.

"Tell me where he is!"

"Sebastián, stop it!" Mami said. "Why don't we call the police?"

"No," Celia said, shaking her head. "The police never believe us. They don't—they never—"

"Let me fix it, Celia."

"You *can't!*"

"Let go of her, Sebastián."

"No!" Papi yelled. "No one gets away with anything anymore!"

"But you can't just—"

"Tell me!"

"No!"

Papi squeezed Celia's wrist and she screamed. The windows must have shaken. Abuelo covered his ears with his hands.

"*Por Dios*, stop hurting her like that!" Abuelo said.

"Where is he?"

"The Hotel Nacional."

"What room?"

"211."

Papi let go of her, and I saw him decide something within himself. He strode towards the door.

"Where are you going?" Mami said.

"I'm going to find him."

"Why don't we tell Rodrigo? He'll do something."

"No," Papi said. "This is for me to do. *Adiós*, Deianeira."

Celia screamed, "He'll kill you! He'll kill you all!"

Papi closed the screen door. The headlights of Abuelo's car lit up. They rushed away, as innocent as fireflies in the dark, past the windows and the curtains and the paint-chipped houses of Marianao. And I had no trouble imagining those headlights travelling up the driveway in Vedado that was lined with palm trees, pulling up next to the limousines and the sleek black cars. I could see it all—the reds and whites and yellows of the lobby with its glass sliding doors and its fancy suitcases and its bellhops, and *los americanos* who didn't know of Papi in his blue old man's car with death in his heart for whoever happened to be in room 211, or of Miguel who had almost been blown to pieces there a few weeks before.

Celia wiped her eyes, and was small in the indent Papi had left in the couch.

"I should never have come here," she said, "He's as good as dead."

Pingüino picked up the dominoes and I helped him, both of us on our knees, coconut water soaking into my dress. I found Papi's glass and I righted it on the carpet, though it was empty now. We found the box (the top of it had the Cuban flag etched into the lid) and placed in the dominoes one by one, stacked up like a pile of yellowed shining teeth. In the kitchen, Mami muttered to herself about bandages. Abuelo went to the television and turned the volume up with a twist of the knob, where a newsman talked about the weather (*"Mañana, un poco de lluvia con temperaturas en los ochentas…"*), and then sat in his chair.

As we slid the wooden lid over the dominoes, Celia watched the newsman on the television.

"He's as good as dead," she whispered, to herself this time, as if she were the only person in the room.

24.

Todo y Todo el Mundo

"I'm not trash if that's what you're thinking."

I was scared she might've been talking to me (I had been gazing off toward the dresser at the picture of Mami on the front steps with her wedding dress, wondering where she kept it hidden), but it didn't take long for me to realize that she was talking to Mami, who was sitting in the chair across from Abuelo's. Abuelo had gone to try and put Pingüino to bed because it was getting late, and Mami didn't want him to stay up waiting for someone who might not come back. Celia took turns holding the wet rag to her lip and then to her eye. There were dark finger marks across her throat as if a ghost were choking her.

"I didn't say anything," Mami said.

"I know when someone's judging me. You think I'm trash."

"I have nothing to say to you."

"Deianeira—"

"Don't call me that."

"What?"

"Call me Doña Deianeira."

"Is it because I'm black?"

"*What?*"

"That you think I'm trash."

Mami stared at her.

125

"You can admit it, if you like. I think it helps. Well, sometimes. For example: I think you are repressed and judgmental."

"*Por Dios*, is your sole purpose in life to make everyone around you uncomfortable?"

"Someone's got to do it. Otherwise, there's no truth."

Mami buried her head in her hands. "Why did this have to happen to me?"

"I don't know."

"The question was rhetorical."

"I hate those. They never have any answers."

"What is *wrong* with you?"

"People have been asking me that a lot lately."

"You're awfully calm."

"I'm really not, you know. Everything feels like it's happening too fast and I don't"—Celia took a deep breath—"I don't know how to *be* right now."

Mami sighed. She gazed at the floor for a long while before speaking. "I don't know what to do either," she said, "He's going to get arrested or worse. I don't even know how this happened."

Celia was silent, gazing at the floor also.

"Who did this to you?" Mami said.

"The less you know the better."

"Is he a policeman?"

"No. He's a mobster. An American."

"This is going to ruin everything."

We watched the television uselessly.

"If he's a client," I said, "then why…?"

"Why did I say no?" Celia said, finishing my sentence. She wasn't surprised. I could tell Mami was disturbed I'd asked.

"Because I don't want this anymore. I got into it because when my parents died, Dulce and I were sixteen and fourteen and we needed jobs. We'd been sleeping in our Titi Sandra's Laundromat, but then she died and we needed money. Dulce hated it. She never told anyone except me because it wasn't something you were supposed to admit to. Then one night one of her clients got rougher than usual, and she quit. She couldn't do it anymore. She would show up to a job and start crying before anybody had even touched her. Lucky for her she got that job at the Zapatería de Cuba, otherwise she might've cracked. I've never looked for anything else because I was okay with myself. It was only when I met your father that I realized I wasn't very happy, that I started thinking maybe I could be something different. But the man who did this to me, I've known him for years, and normally he's nice, he doesn't treat me like the others, except this time I realized I didn't want to do it anymore and I told him I didn't want to, but he wouldn't listen and he just kept saying '*Dale dale* it's okay, gorgeous, Imma take care of you, gorgeous' but I told him no and he just grabbed me by the hair and…"

And then she wasn't calm anymore and she started crying again.

"I'm sorry," she said. "I'm so sorry."

"Celia," I said. "Are you saying Dulce was…?"

Celia nodded.

"And you were fourteen when you started?"

Celia nodded again.

"How old are you exactly?" Mami asked, and there was no tenderness in her voice.

Celia chuckled, and the sound of it was ugly through the tears, "There you go. I said it, didn't I? Judgmental. To the core."

I felt bad for her. She had no one. She didn't have a mother or an aunt or a sister to wrap their arms around her as she wept. And I could almost see how she could convince herself that someone like Papi might love her, to save her from having to return alone to her sagging old mattress and her decrepit gray building with laundry lines hanging out of the window. I wished she had someone other than Mami whose eyes held no sympathy, and me whose arms would never be enough, and how could they be with what she'd been through?

And yet she had ruined everything. I knew she was young and naïve and probably didn't know any better, but still I was angry at the way things had played out. I couldn't even understand how Papi had picked Celia over Mami, how he could ignore the life they had built and choose someone like Celia instead. She had had the nerve to barge into our house twice and look Mami in the eye and demand that the universe align itself for her, and here was the result. Mami, Celia, and I together in the half-light waiting for everything to fall apart. Papi in Abuelo's car travelling to Vedado in the nighttime.

I thought about what Miguel had said, about how the mobsters at the Hotel Nacional didn't have their guns with them, and I hoped to God it was true. Abuelo came back and the exhaustion in his eyes told us how things had gone with Pingüino. He returned to his green chair and I sat on the arm of it. Soon a tortuous hour had passed, and it was like Miguel and the Hotel Nacional all over again, except this time it was Papi and it was all Celia's fault. My eyes felt heavy, but I pinched myself on the shoulder every time I felt myself drifting. Celia cried sometimes, and in the more quiet moments stared vacantly at the wall, perhaps thinking of the suffering she had caused, although I didn't think so. Abuelo fell asleep and I moved to the chair next to Mami, her college diary gleaming on her lap. On the television, a telenovela played, but none of us watched. We let the light wash over our faces, knowing we were all thinking the same thing: *Why isn't he back yet?*

Papi lying dead in the street over the cobblestones.

Why isn't he back yet?

Papi bullet-ridden, his corpse floating in the turquoise pool.

Why isn't he back yet?

Papi with his throat slit, his neck bleeding into the pillow.

Why isn't he back yet?

Or…

Stop it, I told myself.

2:30 in the morning. A clattering of the lock. Mami grabbed hold of my hand. The door creaked open.

Papi. Stone-faced. A splatter of red on his shirt, another on his forehead. His fists hung at his sides, and they were bruised like the knuckles of the stranger who'd punched Luis. He said nothing. Celia stood. Abuelo snored, glasses askew. Everyone stared at one another. Mami rushed towards him and fussed at the gash on his forehead, the blood on his clothes. "What did you do? Are you hurt? I can't believe—"

Papi watched her. I imagined he might have wanted to hold her but didn't know how. Celia lingered by the couch, uncomfortable with herself.

"Is he dead?" she said.

"No."

"That was stupid of you."

"I didn't want to kill him."

"He won't leave you alone. His cars will be up and down this street within the next few days and one day you'll come home to the

129

windows shattered. You have to run. Pack everything as fast as you can and get out of here. You can't tell your friends, you can't tell your neighbours. Just take everything and go. *Todo y todo el mundo.* Everything and everyone."

My stomach dropped. *Everything.* Everything was falling apart. I tried thinking about all those things I had ever known, all those things I would have to say goodbye to. But I couldn't. It was just a white buzzing, a big blank. And in that big white buzzing blank, Celia's words rebounded and cascaded and grew louder and softer over and over again—*todo, todo, todo, everything, everything, everything…*

"Everything?" Mami said sharply, and something told me she knew of the big white buzzing blank also, could hear it crumbling all around her shoulders, "Are you sure? How do you know?"

"I've known him long enough to understand how he works. You have to get out of Havana as soon as you can."

"But won't he follow us?"

"He's an American. He won't stray far."

Mami was pale like she wanted to throw up in the sink, "Where will we go?"

"Anywhere," Celia said.

"I'll send a letter to Noelia at the plantation," Papi said. "I'll tell her to be ready in a week."

"Oriente?"

"We need to get away from here."

"But that's where Fidel is. And what about Pingüino and Adela? Don't think there are any schools there I'd send them to, and… Sebastián, we've been here so long. How can we leave?"

"You're going to have to," Celia said.

"Oh, why did you have to do it?" Mami cried.

"What's done is done," Papi said.

"But you didn't even think." It slipped out of my mouth quiet and soft. I barely knew it existed. The whole room paused. Abuelo's snoring sifted in the air.

"What do you mean I didn't think?"

"You didn't think about us."

"Adela—"

"You lied when you said you loved Mami, didn't you?"

"What?"

"You don't care about her. You don't care about any of us."

Papi was speechless.

"What about me and Pingüino? Were we never enough?"

"Of course, you're enough, you were always—"

"No we weren't. We never were. You don't even know us."

"How can you say that?"

Suddenly the big white buzzing blank snapped into place, and it came to me, the world I would have to say goodbye to. Pingüino and I sitting on the wall of el Malecón with the waves crashing behind us. We were old and wrinkled like Abuelo and we ate popcorn by the sea. The sky was red and pink and orange all at once like layers of sherbert the way it always was at sunset in Havana, the way it had been our whole lives. We had grown up in our small blue house in Marianao and gone to school at the University of Havana and married and had children and our grandchildren played on the cobblestone of the walkway, feeding the pigeons. There were teenagers drinking wine from cartons and old African ladies selling rosaries from booths. It came to me so vividly, the Havana of my mind. I could taste the salt of the popcorn burning my tongue, could

131

smell the heavy sweat-scent of the ocean. That Havana was mine and it would always be mine, except it wasn't. Because it wasn't just things I would have to say goodbye to, but an entire future, an entire possibility of life I could have had if it weren't for Papi. He had taken his boredom and dissatisfaction and plunged blind into his so-called survival and in the process he had re-routed our lives. And maybe he was sorry. And maybe he meant it. But he wasn't sorry for us. He wasn't sorry for our house in Marianao or the shoe shop in Havana or our kitchen with the walls painted orange. He wasn't sorry for Mami who had given so much, or Pingüino who didn't know so many things, or me who felt so ignored I felt like I was dissolving. He was sorry for himself. He was sorry for himself and no one else. I was crying and I hadn't even realized it, "I hate you."

Papi's eyes dimmed, and there was a long silence. He opened his mouth a few times to speak, but didn't. He had run out of ways to justify himself. Papi stared at his own hands and blinked. Then he walked away.

"Where are you going?" Mami said.

"To take a shower."

"But what do we do?"

"We'll pack in the morning," Papi said, then disappeared into the hallway.

"I'm staying," Celia said.

"Says who?" Mami said.

"Deianeira—"

Mami cut her off with a look. Celia tried again.

"Doña Deianeira. He knows where I live. I can't go home tonight. I want to help."

Mami closed her eyes.

"Please," Celia said. And even though it wasn't all her fault and it never could be, I hated the fact she was still here and that she had spoken. Mami looked at her.

"Fine," she snapped. "I'm not in control anyway. You can sleep on the couch if you want. My father will probably get up in the middle of the night and wander back to his room, so don't worry about him and…" Mami sighed as if she couldn't believe she had to say it to her husband's mistress in her own living room filled with her furniture, and the pictures of her children, and all the things she had accumulated over the past thirteen years… "*Buenas noches*, Celia."

"*Buenas noches*, Doña Deianeira."

Celia picked up the bloody rag and it unpeeled itself from the floor with a wet squelch. She began washing it in the sink. The dripping of the water echoed in the night. Mami hugged me and wiped the tears from my cheeks.

"In the morning a new day," she told me. "As for your father messing up the beautiful things in life, the only advice I can give you is…" She glanced at Celia who was wringing water from the towel, and whispered it like a secret, "*Never get married.*"

25.
Three Days

Three days. That's all it took. Our entire lives in Marianao packaged in a mere ten boxes. We piled them by the front door so that when night fell, we'd carry them to Abuelo's car, one by one, so the neighbours wouldn't talk. It wasn't everything. Just the essentials. Mami's pots and pans with the brown grizzle on the bottoms. Pingüino's old baseball bat. Papi's piggy bank that his father had given him when he'd gone off to college. Rubia, my stuffed bunny with the pink ribbon Tía Carmen had given me as a baby. The journal I drew flowers in, even though there were only a couple of pages left.

All of the pictures on the dresser were swept up at once, piled into a box along with a few odds and ends; Pingüino's baby shoes, our childhood drawings, Mami's diary from college. Mami wanted to take the lamp, but Papi wouldn't let her. Then, clothing for everyone. Papi's church clothes and Mami's yellow flower print dress. The school uniforms Pingüino and I had used for years though we knew deep down, as we folded them and rubbed out the creases, that we would never use them, or any other school uniform, ever again. A pair of shoes for each of us, all of them made in Papi's shop. We picked them based on memory rather than convenience. All the furniture was to be left behind, including Abuela's old dressing table and Abuelo's green armchair. Mami's makeup was to be left in the drawers, Papi's heavy dress suit in the closet.

Celia stayed in the house all three days, and every day she stood in the living room, piling stuff into sections and helping Mami decide what got to stay and what got to go. It was surreal watching them work together. I expected Mami to explode any moment, but she stayed quiet, eyes faraway and blank—except for when Celia went to another room to get something, and Mami would look at her with such hatred I wondered how Celia didn't notice. On the first day, Celia had these two determined creases in her chin, and she pretended like her clothes weren't torn, her lip wasn't cut, her hair wasn't a mess. The two of them in the living room, passing things around, one after the other, like an assembly line. And Pingüino and I would help wordlessly hours on hours on end after school, because Papi said that pulling us out might be "suspicious" and people might "start to wonder what was going on".

At Tío Rodrigo's house, things were just the same. Sometimes Pingüino and I went over to their house to help, and they had even fewer things to pack up than we did. Tía Carmen had her collection of old mint cans in the cabinet above the bathroom sink that we persuaded her to throw away. Tío Rodrigo had his police certification in an old glass frame, the paper on the inside filled with indecipherable cursive and a faded coffee ring on the bottom right corner. Miguel packed all of his things up within two hours, in an old suitcase of his father's whose zippers got stuck midway through.

Miguel had been thinking about what he would pack for a long time: "All I need are my hot posters of Elizabeth Taylor, my baseball stuff, a few changes of clothes, and a few bottles of Coca-Cola. Everything else can burn for all I care. Adela, I'll admit that Tío Sebastián cheating on Tía Deianeira is about one of the worst things I've ever heard of. But I can't tell you how happy I am to get out of this neighbourhood. I'm tired of walking down the streets scared of bombs and guns on the way to work. I want to get away from the Hotel Nacional and its stupid smiling *americanos*. And now that I know that one of them's the reason we've got to clear out, I'm not sorry if I can put miles between me and that place… There are some things we'll miss though, won't we? Like riding our bikes and talking about crazy Luis Rodríguez…" He paused. "The other downside, I guess, is that we'll never know if Anita comes back, will we? No one's going to know what happened to us. Maybe they'll think we were kidnapped too. Maybe Anita'll come back and we'll be the ones gone for a change."

Before I could think of how to respond, Miguel continued: "But I guess it wouldn't matter then because everyone would be okay even if they didn't know it. And hey—maybe life's better on the other side, you know? Maybe wherever we're going there'll be plenty of *chicas hermosas,* pretty girls to go after. There certainly aren't any in this town, I'll tell you that. It's not like I haven't looked." And he smiled, but the smile didn't reach his eyes.

As for Pingüino, things had been rough. He no longer talked about Sister Juana or how much he hated school, and he hadn't even said anything about the possibility of never going to one again. Instead night after night it was conversations of "Will they ever be nice to each other again?" and "Why is Celia here? Why do they let her stay?" and sometimes barely any words at all. Just the both of us lying flat on our backs, counting down the hours we had left in this place, in this bedroom, the only place we'd ever slept in our entire lives. And even with everything going on, Havana and Marianao bustled on. There were still gunshots pop-pop-popping at night, though we were no longer as scared of them. There were still people getting groceries. There was still Doña Theresa waving to us whenever she saw us, and Don Manolo smoking log-like cigars from the comfort of his front porch. Papi still shined his shoes in the mornings. Mami still cleaned the dishes and did the laundry. Abuelo still sat in his green chair and watched television.

One day, I noticed Abuelo standing sad in a corner, observing as everything was dismantled. Celia and Mami had taken a quick fifteen-minute break to drink glasses of water that sweat in the heat, and soon they were back at it, cleaning out the contents of the kitchen cabinets this time—old cans of beans and rusted whisks and the pan Mami had used to make a turkey one Christmas a couple of years ago. And Abuelo did nothing but watch. Half his body disappeared into the curtains, white with green stencilling. I half-expected them to swallow him whole, for him to vanish in a pale swish of fabric.

"Abuelo. What are you thinking?"

Abuelo sighed, and rubbed his eyes beneath his glasses. "About how hard it is to build things up. And how easy it is to tear them apart."

He touched his hands to the curtains as if he expected them to stay put, but they floated away, just out of reach. The sunlight dappled them into ghosts.

"Your *abuela* made these curtains three weeks before she died," Abuelo said. "She was too skinny for her favourite dress at the end. Before she got sick, she used to wear it all the time, with these white pair of sandals I had made special at the shoe shop for her birthday, and they were so worn on the bottoms the soles were peeling off. The day she cut up the dress, the whole house was so quiet you could hear every snip of the scissors. She could hardly use her fingers to sew the fabric together, they were shaking so much, but she was determined to be done with that old thing. Taunting her in the closet every morning about the way she used to be. The first time seeing the bits of dress hung up by the window, it was like seeing a dead animal hung up to dry. Like Adela had strung a bit of herself up there to die before the rest of her did."

Abuelo took a bunch of curtain, and held it tightly in his fist, making deep, violent creases.

"I don't want to leave you behind, Adela." His voice broke. "I don't want to. But I have to. You won't be happy in the countryside, and I couldn't do that to you. I won't move you, I won't."

The blood rushed through my head. "Me?"

"No, I mean her. Her."

He stared vacantly at the white-and-green fabric. "*Mi* Adela, *mi pobre* Adela…"

26.

As Meaningless as Shoes

In all the time we spent packing, I only saw Papi and Celia together once. They were on the front porch and the sun was setting. Mami was dealing with the porcelain and I was helping her pack it all into boxes with leftover tissue paper from the shoe shop. The table in the kitchen had been moved to make more room, and we were sitting on the floor with bits of paper scattered all around us. The orange of the walls reflected the light of the sunset and it bounced around the room and settled onto the paper as if we were stranded in a valley of orange peels.

"Are you sure we have to pack this?" I asked.

"Yes," Mami said. "I spent a lot of money on it."

"I know. I wanted some *pastelitos* from the Panadería and you bought dusty old porcelain from the antique shop instead."

Mami laughed. "And your father was furious with me for buying them, but we put them to good use anyway, didn't we? All those Christmas Eves..." She wrapped a glass with a chip in it and put it at the bottom of the box.

"Mami," I said. "How can you be okay with this?"

"With what?"

"All of this."

"You mean your father?"

I nodded. She smiled sadly. "I'm not."

"But you seem fine."

"Well. I'm not."

"Mami, I think really I hate him."

"Don't say that."

"But it's true."

"No, it isn't."

"Don't you?"

"Sometimes I think I do. But no—I don't hate him."

"I don't understand how we're supposed to keep living with him."

"*Mijita*, if I could do something about that I would, but I can't. We're just going to have to start seeing things differently."

"How?"

"I don't know. Things are hard right now, but it'll get better."

"What if it doesn't?"

"It will. It has to."

"I'm scared."

"I know, *bebe*," she said, and she touched my hair. "So am I."

"What about school? You said you wouldn't let us go."

"I'll teach you. Both of you. There'll be more people at the plantation anyway, more people to do the jobs I used to do. I think it's time other people did some of the cooking for a change."

"But what about…?"

"What?"

I hesitated before saying it. "What about university?"

"What about it?"

"Can I go?"

Mami thought about it a moment. "I don't know. We'll see."

"But how would we… how would we even…"

"I don't know, Dela. But we can try and figure it out."

There was a strangely happy pause.

"Thank you."

"You're welcome," she said, and she smiled.

I wrapped a plate in paper and placed it in a box, and Mami did the same with a glass.

"If you're not going to cook, does that mean no more *ropa vieja*?"

"No, I'll make it for you, Dela. But it'll be because I want to. Besides, I don't think life in Oriente will be so bad. I might even dance again."

"Really?"

"Really."

"I still hate him."

"That will change."

"How do you know?"

"I don't," Mami said. "I don't know a lot of things."

The sky dimmed.

"Can I take a break?"

"Sure. But don't take too long. There are still things to do."

I walked into the living room, and saw them. Papi and Celia on the front porch. The sight of them made something inside me recoil because I couldn't believe they could be so stupid after everything that had happened to continue speaking to each other. They were sitting on the top step together, and Celia had the white box between them, the white box with the red shoes. The door was propped open and I could hear them speaking quietly.

"I thought you wanted them?" Papi said.

"I did, but I don't anymore. They're beautiful."

"I want you to keep them. They're yours."

"I know, it's just…"

"What?"

"I don't need a reminder."

"It's not your fault, you know. It's mine."

"No, it's his. Not us. Him."

"Won't he come after you?"

"It's fine, don't worry about it."

"Are you sure?"

"I know him. Trust me."

"How can you say that after what he did to you?"

"I—I don't know. Please, I don't want to talk about it anymore."

A pause.

"You can come with us if you like."

Celia hesitated. "There's no room in the car."

"You can take the train. That's how my brother and his family are getting out."

"No one will want me where you're going. The best thing for me to do is forget, and I can't do that if you don't take the shoes back."

"Please, Celia. Keep them."

Celia searched Papi's face. "I can't have them."

"Yes, you can. I want you to have them."

"Please, I—"

"No. You're keeping them. Not because you want to, but because I'm asking you to. Here." Papi placed the box in her lap.

She placed her hands on the box and stared at her fingers. "Okay," she said finally. "I'll keep them... But only because they won't mean anything. They'll be shoes and nothing more."

Papi gazed at her. "Of course."

"When are you leaving?"

"The day after tomorrow. Early in the morning."

"Haven't you finished packing?"

"Yes, but I need to find someone to take care of the shoe shop, and my brother needs to get his last paycheck from the police department. Then we leave."

"Oh."

"Will you be there?"

"What?"

"Will you be there to say goodbye?"

"I don't think that's a good idea."

"Tomorrow night. Just to say goodbye."

"Sebastián…"

"Please."

Celia sighed and stared at the sky. "Fine. But no funny business. Just goodbye and nothing more. As meaningless as the shoes."

"As meaningless as the shoes," Papi agreed.

Celia replaced the lid on the box with the shoes in it. She stood. "Goodbye, Don Sebastían."

"This isn't goodbye. Tomorrow is."

"I know, but for now it is. Goodbye." She kissed him on the cheek. She stepped off the porch. She walked away. Past Rafi Consuelo's house and Don Manolo's house and the intersection between them. Past the allamanda bush and the spot where the dog had died with its eyes rolling the year before. She kept walking until she was a speck in the distance and then she turned into oblivion.

27.

Luces

After Celia left, night blushed its darkness across the sky, a thimble-full of silver pinpricks bleeding their way through. Miguel, Pingüino, and I had never gathered on the front porch at night, but I suppose it didn't matter anymore. This first would be our last. We had cleared out everything from the refrigerator except for a gallon of milk, and Mami told us we had to get rid of it. So we put it on the top step, taking swigs from it and not bothering with glasses. We drank from it silently, like family.

The mosquitoes were out. They bit at us every few minutes, and every few minutes one of us would smack ourselves hard across the bumps forming on our arms and legs. I got a mosquito bite the size of a coin at the base of my index finger and I scratched it until it bled.

"Did Tío Rodrigo tell you why the two strangers were arrested?" I asked Miguel.

"No. He doesn't talk about work. He told us he'd arrested them, but he wouldn't give us their names or why they'd been arrested. Things have gotten worse since then. He comes in late more often and panics in the bathroom. Let's just say it's hard to find somewhere to take a piss nowadays."

"He panics in the bathroom?" Pingüino asked.

Miguel nodded, and didn't explain. He took a swig from the gallon of milk.

"I never told you guys about the last time I saw Luis Rodríguez, did I?" I said.

"No!" Pingüino said, "No, you did not tell us about 'the last time you saw Luis Rodríguez.' When was this? *Por Dios*, Adela you've been holding out on us."

"I'm with Pingüino on this one," Miguel said, "Spill the beans, *prima*."

"Well, I went over there on Sunday after... you know, after the first time Celia came to the house. It was while everyone else was at church, and you, Pingüino, were sleeping, no help at all, and I went over there to return the glasses and spoons we'd taken from Doña Theresa's house the week before. Luis opened the door and he was in pretty bad shape—had this big bruise on his cheek and a gash on his forehead. He told me it was those two strangers who'd done it. And then he said all these weird things like 'Please forgive me' and 'I did the right thing' and 'Do you like President Batista?' Then he grabbed me and said something about not regretting whatever he'd done. So I ran out of there as fast as I could."

Another mosquito bit my neck, and I smacked at it.

"Jesus, Adela," Miguel said. "And you forgot to mention this?"

I shrugged. "A lot of things happened after that with Celia. I forgot."

"Like I said," Pingüino huffed, "All the fun stuff happens to Adela."

"It wasn't fun at all. He could've done anything to me and no one would've known. He could've slit my throat and buried me under the lemon trees and that would've been the end of it."

"Adela, *por favor*," Pingüino said, "We all know Luis Rodríguez wouldn't do something like that..." Miguel was uncertain in the dark. "Would he?"

Miguel took another swig from the gallon of milk. "It doesn't matter," he said flatly. "We won't ever know. By the end of the week, we'll be far away and never coming back."

"*Dios mío*, you say that like it's a good thing," Pingüino said, "Aren't you even a little bit sad?"

Miguel was silent a moment, his face inscrutable. "No."

"I can't believe it's happening," I said. "I keep seeing all the boxes piled into the back of Abuelo's car, and it feels like we're going on vacation somewhere and we'll be back soon. Like we're just going to the beach for a few days, packing up towels and swimsuits and extra clothes and sandals and getting sand all over the car, but we'll be back. But we're not. We're leaving. Forever."

"Hmm," Pingüino said. He gazed at the pinpricks in the sky. I could see a mosquito bite the shape of a torpedo on his elbow. He took the jug of milk and tried swigging it like Miguel had. Except he tilted it too far and it spewed everywhere. Milk squirted out of Pingüino's mouth and it sounded like air being let out of a balloon too fast. "*¡COJONES!*" he screamed, and Miguel and I laughed.

"It's not funny!" Pingüino said. He grabbed his nose and his voice came out nasally, "*Ay, mierda*, I think some of it went up my nose."

We laughed so hard tears poured down our cheeks. Miguel kept pounding his fist on the top step of the porch, struggling for breath.

"I could have died!" Pingüino cried. "Would you be laughing then?"

"Yes," I said, wheezing.

And Miguel and I, we laughed in a way we hadn't laughed in a long time—the last time had been when Miguel told us the story of when he'd tried to flirt with some French girl on Paseo del Prado in Havana. She was brunette, wore sunglasses in the shape of butterfly wings, spoke snatches of Spanish with guttural French Rs, and was drop-dead gorgeous, and he'd farted by accident while telling her she reminded him of the sun. We laughed then like we laughed now. Until our faces were red and the air in our lungs had been leaked out, and we were reduced to weak giggling, stranded like beached fish on the porch.

Pingüino went still. The milk jug was abandoned at the top step. "Adela. Miguel."

His voice snagged at me, and I stopped laughing.

"What?" I said. "What is it?"

"There," Pingüino said, and he pointed behind us. "Tell me you see it too."

Miguel and I turned.

The lights in Rafi Consuelo's house were blazing again. I waited for them to snap out of existence like last time, but they wouldn't. They went on shining as if they knew we were watching and wouldn't settle for being predictable.

"I see it," Miguel said. "I actually see it."

"Ha!" Pingüino said. But there was a lilting uncertainty in his voice as he said it. "I saw it first!"

"*Cállate*, Pingüino," I said, "What do we do?"

"I'll tell you what we do," Miguel said. He stood. "We're going over there."

"Are you crazy?" I said, "I thought you were okay with not knowing."

"That's what I said when I thought we didn't have a choice. But the lights are on again, Adela. It's now or never. Either we go over there or we never know. Is that really what you want?"

"But what about the police? Or Tío Rodrigo? Shouldn't we tell them?"

"Come on, we know what happens then. The lights go out, the police take over, and we never know. Or they lie about it. Do you really think everything they say is true? Aren't you sick of all the lies, Adela? Aren't you sick of all the things we aren't allowed to talk about? Just once, Adela, I'd like to be free. Let's be free. The three of us together. What do you say?"

"I don't think this is a good idea, Miguel."

"And what about you Pingüino? In or out?"

Pingüino drew himself up taller. His shirt was soaked in milk, and some of it clung to his face, "In."

"Please, Adela," Miguel said.

I studied Rafi Consuelo's house and the glaring white glow behind the curtains. No more lies. No more secrets. Just take the house apart wall by wall until it was rooms and furniture and picture frames and whoever stood inside flicking light switches on and off, stranded in the open. We would be eyes in the sky, peering in through the rooftops.

"Okay," I said. "I'll do it."

Together, we stepped away from the familiar circle of yellow alley-light glow that embraced our porch every night. Together, we barrelled into the mosquito-filled darkness, on toward the whiteness flooding from Rafi Consuelo's resurrected house.

28.
Dead Man

Rafi Consuelo's doorknob was rusted, and we stared at it, daring each other to be the first to touch it, but no one would. Rafi Consuelo had a doormat and it was soaked with old rain, squelching beneath our feet as we shifted back and forth. It was the same night, the same darkness, the same white-glow behind Rafi Consuelo's shutters. But it felt different on this side of things. Right there in front of us. A twist of the doorknob away.

The lights went out.

"*Coño*, did you see that?" Pingüino said.

"*Shhh!*" Miguel said, "What if someone hears you?"

There was a tightness in my chest. I tried the doorknob. It was old and rusted. It grated as it gave, and the door swung open into empty air. A hush fell over us and, one by one, we stepped in. Miguel first. Pingüino second. Me last. We blinked, our eyes creating shapes out of layers of shadow. Then a face loomed from the dark.

"Close the door."

"Rafi, is that you?" Pingüino said, rubbing his eyes.

"Close the damn door right now."

Objects in the room took form one by one. First, the walls adorned with street art, the kind tourists bought—pictures of beaches and palm trees, and sexy showgirls shaking maracas, and women with flowers in their hair. Then the floors came into view. They were covered in crumpled newspapers with headlines from weeks before ("Batista Smashes Armed Revolt," "Bomb Goes Off on the Grounds of Hotel Nacional") along with old cigar butts and half-blackened matchsticks and mostly empty glasses of rum, some of it spilled sticky and old at the corner of the room, a swarm of ants swimming half-dead. The next thing was the patched-up couch that could have only belonged to a college student, to someone who had found it on the side of a highway exit somewhere. Then—what was on the couch and scattered around it.

I counted five machine guns. Sleek and shining, but peaceful in the way they were tossed on the ground, slung over the back of the couch by their straps like women's bags. More than a dozen rifles also, too many to count, with broad wooden bases leaning against the back wall. The handguns were in a haphazard pile, four of them, nested atop a bundle of clothing I recognized as Havana police uniforms, their bright blue stranded on the floor oddly as if pieces of noonday sky had unpeeled themselves and fallen to earth. And then, rounds and rounds of ammunition. Gold-headed and linked together, each one a miniature of Mami's tubes of red lipstick. Great strings of them laid out on the couch, deadly Christmas garlands meant to be wrapped around a tree, garrotte-like.

And after all that—after the posters, the crumpled newspapers, the cigarettes, the matchsticks, the old rum, the battered couch, the weapons shining sinister in starlight—was the face itself, the one that had spoken. Its glasses. Its awkward black moustache. The nervous fidgetiness of its eyes. It was a man and he was pointing a handgun at my chest.

"Luis?"

"*Hola*, Adela," Luis Rodríguez said.

"What is all this?"

"Fidel, of course," Luis said, and he sounded bitter, "What did you think it was?"

A moment of silence as we absorbed everything—the room, the weapons, Luis Rodríguez, the very real gun pointed at us. Pingüino's grip tightened around my hand, and I feared the tips of my fingers might be blue.

"The Presidential Palace," Miguel said. "That was you wasn't it?"

"What? No."

"Then what are all these weapons for?"

"It's a weapons cache."

"Do you know where Anita is?"

"No."

"Okay. Rafi. What about Rafi?"

"I don't know where any of them are."

"Are they dead? Did you kill them?"

"Whatever you think I did, that's not—I didn't—"

"What did you do?" I said.

"I've made a horrible mistake."

"I thought you said you did the right thing."

"I know—I thought—I let them get to my head, and I shouldn't have."

"I don't know what you're talking about. Luis, please let us go. We won't tell anyone, we promise. We'll just leave this house, and you can leave the lights off and no one will ever know, okay? Can you— Can you put down the gun, please?"

"Adela, do you know what Cuba is?" he said as if he hadn't heard me.

I kept my mouth shut.

"It's people dragging their lives behind them, but no one cares who's in charge. And if one day America or Batista or somebody decides to fuck with our city, turn streets into brothels, and have murderers run the economy, do you know what those people do? They go on. They go on and they pretend like nothing's happening and maybe—that's what they think in their heads—maybe things will turn out all right. Don't make a fuss and I can go on living, that's what they think. But what about everyone else? What about those shirtless kids in the slums by the baseball stadium? What they get is hell, *la casa del carajo*. No one does anything and that's what Cuba is right now.

"Fidel… *por Dios* maybe you're too young to understand this, but Fidel knows. He knows what's wrong. He sees these people, these poor people banished to *la casa del carajo* for no good reason, and he wants to fix it. And in the beginning that's why I did what I did. *Los americanos* there lounging by their goddamn pool in their goddamn hotel because Havana is just their playhouse, because all they think we are are funny people speaking a funny language, and by God, I thought, by God they'd understand—"

"Wait," Miguel said. "That was you? You bombed the Hotel?"

"Are you Miguel?"

"Yes."

"I used to know you when I was younger. Maybe you don't remember. It was baseball. In the field by the Catholic School. You were so small you couldn't play yet, and I remember your mother used to yell at you because you liked running your hands through the dirt and getting your pants dirty."

Miguel was caught off-guard, "You almost killed me."

"No, I didn't mean for that to happen. I just—It was an idea I had.

152

It was before coming here. It was me and Jorge and Pablo—the two men you met at church a few weeks ago—and we were on the train together coming back from the Sierra Maestra, from months of sweating in the jungles and learning how to shoot at people from far away and the train ride was just the three of us talking about *los americanos* and how they thought we were so small and how they went inside their spotless cages in hotels like the Hotel Nacional and refused to know about the suffering they caused. And how Batista loved those cages so much, how he sent all of his favourite rich people and mobsters and celebrities there like goddamn Frank Sinatra and goddamn Meyer Lanksy. And I said, I told them, 'Wouldn't it be great if we could teach them a lesson? Just bomb the place. Boom. Up in flames. That'd show them, wouldn't it?' And we laughed about it for a bit, but then they got serious, and they talked about our weapons supply at Rafi Consuelo's and rounding up Anita Valle and having a University of Havana reunion, all of us. And if Rafi or Anita opted not to come, then we could just have the party without them. We got here and Rafi wasn't home. We sent a message to Anita, and no response. We thought maybe they'd gone out somewhere, so that night we decided we'd grab what we needed from Rafi Consuelo's, jump into Pablo's car, and throw the bomb over the side of the fence. At night. Poolside. *Los americanos cabrones* wouldn't know what had hit them. That's what we said. And that's what we did… But I understand now it was wrong. I could've hurt you, and the solution to no one trying to fix Cuba's mess isn't hurting the people stuck dragging their lives behind them, because it isn't their fault. And the Americans too, they're ignorant, oblivious. The only thing those people at the Hotel Nacional are guilty of is not knowing, and it's a shame they don't know, but it doesn't mean they should be punished for it. I just wanted to find the people whose fault it was and make them pay. But I don't know whose fault it is. I thought I did, but I'm not sure anymore. I used to think the way it should be done was to get rid of anyone who got in the way, because that's what they taught us in the mountains. But... that night—that night at the Hotel Nacional, I could have killed so many people. That one moment, that bomb soaring in the air, was one of the worst mistakes of my life. And I'm sorry for that, Miguel. I really am."

"So..." Miguel said. "So you really don't know what happened to Anita."

Luis shook his head.

"There's something wrong with you," Miguel said. He was disgusted. "I can't even walk down the street anymore, Luis. It's all shadows and bombs and rebels to me and you did that. You. No one else. You're insane and I feel sorry for you. Sitting here in the dark, in the house of a man who's probably dead, flipping light switches and searching for forgiveness."

"Is that it?" Pingüino said, and I jumped because I'd forgotten he was there, because he was nothing but a sweaty palm grasping mine. "Is that why you turned on the lights?"

"Possibly," Luis said. His eyes were far away. His fingers tightened around the gun. "I didn't do it the first time. It was Jorge and Pablo, fumbling around like idiots and they turned the lights on by accident. They wanted to keep going. They wanted to go back to the Hotel and finish what they'd started. They saw it in the papers, and they didn't think it was good enough. They had a house full of weapons and they wanted to use them. I told them not to and I got beaten for it. They were arrested before they got the chance. Me? I was just sitting here in the dark in the middle of all this. And I promise you, Adela," he said, looking me in the eyes, "I promise you I tried. I really did. But sometimes everything's too big. Sometimes you can't see the small things. And I thought someone ought to know. Someone ought to know before…"

"Before what?" I said.

Luis raised the gun to his temple. He sucked in his breath through his teeth, about to shoot. Pingüino let go of my hand to cover his eyes.

"NO! LUIS, DON'T!" I screamed.

"Why not?" he said, and the tears streamed down his face.

"You didn't even hurt anyone!"

"I almost did. I thought I'd make things better, not worse."

"But that's not how it works, Luis! You said so yourself. It's never perfect and it never could be and it's better that way!"

"No, no," Luis sobbed, the gun pressed against his head.

"You want forgiveness, Luis? Forgive yourself."

"I can't," Luis whispered. "It's not that simple."

"It is, it is, I promise!"

"No, no, it's not. You don't know what goes on in my head, the things I imagine. I've tried to tell myself it doesn't matter, that I can control it, that I can focus on other things, but my head doesn't leave me alone. And it's more than that too—it's not just that I've failed in this, it's that I've failed in everything. All my mother does is sit in her house in her nightgown day after day. I've weighed her down her entire life. I've lived twenty-one years and I have nothing to show for it."

"Luis, please!"

"I'm sorry, Adela. I just… don't want to bother people anymore."

Pingüino had his hand clamped over his eyes and I could hear his breath shuddering in and out, in and out. Luis's finger trembled at the trigger.

"I forgive you." Miguel. His eyes down to the floor.

"What?"

"I forgive you."

Luis's mouth gaped and the tears made tracks alongside it. The tip of the gun was up against his forehead. Suddenly, blue and red lights. They washed across Luis's face, the walls, the couch, the weapons, the trash strewn across the floor. Outside the window, Tío Rodrigo's police car was parked on the street with its lights flashing.

"It's Tío Rodrigo," I said.

Pingüino uncovered his eyes, and Miguel peered out the window. Luis lowered the gun from his forehead, rushed towards us, and pushed us toward the back door. "Run—If they catch you here, they'll take you away and they'll do the same thing as… Lord knows what they're doing to them right now."

"Who?"

"All of them. Rafi and Anita. Jorge and Pablo."

"What? He's my uncle. He wouldn't do anything to us."

"Run," Luis opened the back door and pushed us into the night. "Hide if you have to. Don't let them see."

"But…" I said. "What about you?"

Luis's face was indecipherable. The gun gleamed in his hands.

"*Adiós*, Adela."

The door slammed shut.

29.

Resurrection

All three of us trembled in the bushes. It was the allamanda bush with yellow flowers and green leaves taller than Abuelo's car, and all of it wet from a recent rain, brushing our cheeks and our arms and our hair with water droplets. On my right, Pingüino squatted slightly and his hair touched my shoulder. On my left, Miguel was behind me, his breath fluttering near my ear. We were dead quiet.

Tío Rodrigo clambered up the front steps, as skinny and frail as the last time we'd seen him. The golden centre of his police cap shone. He knocked on the door to Rafi Consuelo's house. The police car was parked on the street and the lights were flashing. The houses up and down the street were oblivious of what went on outside, a few of them with lights behind closed curtains. Tío Rodrigo wasn't alone. Behind him was his partner, Manuel.

"Whoever you are," Tío Rodrigo said. "We know you're in there. Open the door."

He banged on the door. In the distance, a dog howled.

"Open up, or we'll force our way in. I'm giving you until the count of three."

"*Ay mierda, mierda, mierda*," Miguel whispered in my ear. "Luis is still armed. What if he shoots? *Mierda*, he's going to shoot!"

"*¡UNO!*" Tío Rodrigo yelled. "*¡DOS!*" The door was immobile. "*…¡TRES!*"

They barged in and I put my fingers in my ears, waiting to hear pop-pop-popping, except this time it would be right in front of me rather than in a distant alley in Havana, or in the westerns Abuelo watched on the television. The world was muted, my fingernails digging into my ears. It hurt but I didn't care. A few seconds of blood pounding in my ears. Miguel's breath stopped fluttering by my neck. Pingüino had covered his eyes again with his hands.

Luis came out first. He was being pushed, he wasn't struggling. There was no gun. His hands were cuffed behind his back. Manuel held open the door of the police car, and I expected it to be quick and easy, for Tío Rodrigo to push him in, and we'd see the back of Luis's head and then he'd be driven away like the two strangers, perhaps with a tragic look through the back window as he wondered where those three kids went, the ones he'd threatened to kill himself in front of.

Instead—"Manuel, give me a moment. I need to ask Luis a few questions."

It was hard to see through the bushes, but I was pretty sure I saw Manuel raise his eyebrows. I could see the ends of his moustache, his canines a toothpaste-white in the darkness. I unplugged my ears.

"Please. He's my neighbour's son," Tío Rodrigo said.

Manuel hesitated, and then nodded. He retreated to the front seat of the police car. He rolled the windows up. Through the glass, I saw the orange beacon of a cigarette. Tío Rodrigo let go of Luis's arms, and Luis stood free by the back end of the police car, his wrists cuffed.

"You too, huh?" Tío Rodrigo said, "I hate to think what your mother will say tomorrow morning."

"I'm not expecting you to understand," Luis said. "Every few years there's a revolution and it gets crushed, but not this one. You haven't seen it. The base camps. Overflowing with people who are sick and tired of Batista's *mierda*. It'll get to the rest of Cuba soon and it won't be pretty for anyone when it does."

Tío Rodrigo shook his head. "You won't win, Luis. You've already lost."

"Tell me, Don Rodrigo. How bad is it?"

"What?"

"The things they've been doing. To Rafi and Anita and Jorge and Pablo. How bad is it?"

"I don't know what you're talking about. Rafi and Anita have been missing for weeks and there's no sign of them."

Luis laughed. "*Por favor*. Do me the favour of telling me how I'm going to die."

Tío Rodrigo took off his policeman's hat to rub his head in the same way Papi ran his hands through his hair when he was nervous.

"Don Rodrigo," Luis smiled. "There's no one here. It's just you and me and the night sky. And God, of course. My, what must he think of the both of us? Such moral dilemmas. It could take centuries for someone to contemplate them all, but thankfully He has time. And we can't forget Manuel smoking his cigarette in the front seat, although I don't think he can hear us, can he? Just you and me and God. I've been waiting for this, and I know what I'm going to do. I don't plan on talking. I don't plan on spilling. I plan on sitting there silent, screaming when I have to. Because I'm human and I can't help it. So you might as well tell me the truth. How painful is my death going to be?"

The rims of Tío Rodrigo's eyes were red. He sighed, and I recognized it. I recognized it as someone who was fed up with lying about things.

"Very," Tío Rodrigo said. His voice grated with truth. "It's going to be very painful."

"Let me go."

Tío Rodrigo glanced at Manuel's lit cigarette in the front seat. It was dimming fast. "I can't do that, Luis. I'm sorry."

"Do you want this? Do you want any more pain?"

"No. Of course not. I'm tired. So tired I can't breathe."

"Then let me go."

Luis Rodríguez faced the road that led to Don Manolo's house, to the rusted mailboxes, to Havana and all of its white buildings and brothels and bars and restaurants and people and *americanos* and mobsters and citizens sleeping in the slums waiting to wake up to a new day. In his mind's eye, he must have seen the city's glow stretching all the way out to this suburb with its concrete porches and its crumbling streets. A future and a past he could never have. Not anymore.

Tío Rodrigo undid the cuffs. It was a smooth transaction. They faced each other as equals. Eye to eye. Chins up. The rebel and the cop. The mountains and the city. Fidel's soldier and Batista's enforcer. They shook hands on the battlefield, a good strong handshake. I could tell even from behind the leaves and the yellow flowers.

"Are you sure this is what you want?"

"I wasn't sure before," Luis said. I could've sworn Havana's glow rushed in his eyes, heavenly cars travelling on a freeway. "But I am now. I know what I want. I want to be let go."

Tío Rodrigo nodded. "Luis… I set you free."

No dogs barked in the night. No stray voices called from open kitchen windows. No gunshots drifted over from Havana. The light from Manuel's cigarette had gone out, and Manuel was a still, beautiful silhouette, a snapshot. The world was sucked in. Waiting. Patient. It could take its time on this one.

"Goodbye, Don Rodrigo."

He faced Havana once more. He took a deep breath, and his shoulders moved with the exhalation. Then he ran. He ran so that his feet pounded pavement. I could feel the burning with him, the heat on my feet. I could feel the humidity part its way for me like ghosts. I could feel the cleanness of the air tunnelling into my lungs, my chest. I could feel my clothes so light around me it was as if they weren't there at all. I was born again.

Tío Rodrigo removed the gun from his holster. He shot Luis Rodríguez three times and his figure crumpled, the blood across his back like three roses in bloom. On the ground he was a rag doll. One minute a man and the next a rag doll. Pingüino cried. A sharp breath outwards from Miguel. I was silent because I knew I was supposed to be. I was a witness and nothing more.

After Manuel rushed out and got the story from Tío Rodrigo and saw the bloodstains on Luis Rodríguez's shirt, the two policemen piled into the car. They drove away, making a circle around the body as if they were afraid of waking it. The three of us stood in the same place. It was a while before we moved.

It was then that we noticed what lay scattered across the dirt in the bushes, like shattered plates, broken moons. Pingüino's ripped up letter from the principal. It shone creamily in the dirt, and typewritten words jumped out despite everything ("*unbefitting… severely scaring her… third offence… We hope this finds you well…*"), and it was the awful irony of this that forced us away from the allamanda bush with its yellow flowers, from Rafi Consuelo's broken-down door, from Luis's rag-doll body that lay lifeless and bloody in the street. Because even though these things lay heavy in our hearts, there was something to be said for being relieved and guilty that we were still—amazingly—alive.

30.

The Corpses

*FOUR CORPSES FOUND BURIED NEAR CABARET
CONSTRUCTION SITE IN HAVANA*

At 7:30 A.M. this morning, four bodies were found buried beneath six inches of dirt with their eyes open. They were discovered by construction worker Thiago Hernández when digging onsite with a spade and he struck something that felt, as he said, "hard, but not like a rock. Something that was soft on the outside, but hard on the inside." Upon unearthing the dirt further, Hernández observed that what he had struck was an unattached human hand. He kept digging, and found four dead bodies. Three males and a female. All showed signs of torture. All had their fingernails pulled. All had body parts missing, including hands, feet, fingers, and toes. There was no evidence of the fingernails nearby, although the other missing body parts were accounted for.

The police have identified the four victims as former University of Havana students Rafael Consuelo, Pablo Padilla, Jorge Rojas, and Anita Valle. This recent discovery of bodies is one of countless similar cases over the past few years, all with similar characteristics of body mutilation and dismemberment. Just last month, three bodies of known Fidel Castro sympathizers were chopped up and dumped into the sea, discovered only when the parts washed ashore.

At the suggestion these events could be connected, Havana chief of police Esteban Ventura has dismissed any possibility of the events relating to each other. In his official statement concerning the deaths, Ventura has said that the Havana Police Department will "investigate the matter" and that the deaths are "a horrific tragedy, one that will be examined thoroughly." The ages of the deceased are as follows: Rafael Consuelo, 21; Pablo Padilla, 22; Jorge Rojas, 22; Anita Valle, 19.

As for the construction site, plans for the cabaret to be built in this spot have momentarily abated, but will continue within the next week. The discovery of the bodies has had no impact whatsoever on the morale of owner Franklin Ucker who has stated that "while the deaths are certainly unfortunate and I offer my most heartfelt condolences to the families of the victims, I have no plans of terminating construction." The cabaret will open later this fall in November.

It wasn't front-page news, just two columns on the third page of *The Havana Post*. I'm sure everyone on our street was talking about it, or grieving, though none of us would ever know. We were stuck inside for the day, pulled out of school. Luis Rodríguez's body had been cleared from the street. I'd glanced out of the window in the morning and only the bloodstains remained. From afar they could have been anything. Dark oil spills from a car. Tyre marks maybe.

I flipped through the whole newspaper twice and found no mention of Luis Rodríguez or the arms cache in Rafi Consuelo's house. No mention of Tío Rodrigo or his partner, Manuel. No mention of how Rafi and Anita had been missing for a month. No mention of Luis Rodríguez's body stranded in the street with three bullet wounds in his back nor of whoever had made his corpse disappear.

No one cried. No one was surprised. When Papi read the article, he shook his head and said, "That piece of shit, Esteban Ventura. Everyone knows it's him who's cut up those bodies and the newspapers can't even talk about it." When Mami saw the list of the dead, and their ages right next to them, she rubbed her eyes and said, "*Los pobres Valles*. Torturing themselves over whether or not she'd ever come home, and now they know, don't they? Never. Never coming back. She was only nineteen years old. I wonder if the police told them, or if they found out through the newspapers like everyone else." And Abuelo sat in his green chair and muttered to himself, "It's always the people who pay. Real people. Our people this time."

The last box had been packed, and there was no need for Celia anymore. The house seemed strange without her and Mami running through the hallways with lamps or picture frames or radios in their hands, searching for a place to pack things. Instead, Mami watched a televised ballet on the couch and Pingüino sat next to her. Papi shone his shoes in the kitchen, the brush and the towels and the polish strewn about. No one talked.

At one point, Miguel came over and sat in my room, except it wasn't my room anymore because the clothes weren't in the closet and the drawers were hollow with air.

"I think he killed her," Miguel said.

"Anita?"

"Yes."

I remembered Luis lying dead in the road and imagined Tío Rodrigo taking the gun from his holster and shooting her in the back as she ran away. Anita Valle who used to cook and teach us maths and pick us up from school. Anita Valle who used to smile and make us feel like we were worth something. I was sad because I could imagine him doing it. I think Miguel could too. I could imagine everything except her face and that made me even sadder. Miguel looked at the empty closet and there were tears on his face. He turned away from me so I wouldn't see, and I wondered if he remembered her face or if he too had forgotten.

Eventually Miguel went home and Papi went to work. He'd be breaking the news to Dulce about the big move, explaining everything to her. Celia, the mobster at the Hotel Nacional, the plantation in Oriente. He couldn't sell the shoe shop because that would attract too much attention, so he was going to hand it over to Dulce, the whole thing. "She knows how to run it anyway," he said as he went out the door. "To be honest, it's been her doing most of the work. I think she's even better than me at shining shoes. Lord knows she'll be able to keep the place organized." For a few seconds, his eyes went wistful. There would be no more warm gusts of leather wind, no more piles of mutilated shoes at work tables, no more Dulce sitting bored at her desk, flipping through magazines or licking lollipops. Things he'd called mundane. He would be paying the price for it now. I didn't know whether or not he realized it, but I didn't care because I still felt a metal bitterness in my mouth whenever I saw him or heard him speak. What I did know was those few seconds of wistfulness in his eyes. Then out the door, the screen door closing behind him.

31.
Cenizas

At the table, Pingüino and I glanced at each other, waiting for the bubble to burst. Luis Rodríguez was dead and no one knew. To everyone, the stains in the street were oil spills. Tío Rodrigo wasn't a murderer. Luis Rodríguez was sleeping under his own roof. Rafi Consuelo's house remained dead and undisturbed. No one knew the truth except Tío Rodrigo, his partner Manuel, and three kids who had been hiding in the bushes, and knew only how to stay quiet. The bubble needed to burst.

It came in the form of Doña Theresa.

She knocked on the front door and Mami opened it.

"He's dead," Doña Theresa said. "Luis is dead. They killed him."

She was rushed inside and hurried onto the couch. She was given a small cup of coffee, extra sugar, and it shook in her hands as she brought it to her lips.

"Rodrigo came by this morning. He died last night. Right here on our street. In front of Rafi Consuelo's house. I heard three gunshots last night, louder than usual, but I thought they were the normal ones. I thought Luis had gone to the city to meet some friends. I never thought…"

"I'm so sorry," Mami said.

"I'm not even sure I've realized it yet," Doña Theresa said, her voice trembling. "It's not like he's dead, it's more that he's not alive anymore and…" She began to cry and her sobs were heartrending. "Why?— Why did they have to—? *Muerto*—Dead—*Mi pobre* Luis, *mi bebe.*" She screamed with grief.

Abuelo gazed expressionless at her from his chair. Mami sat next to her on the couch and put her arm around her, rubbed her back like a child, waiting for her to calm down enough to speak. It was horrible. It would never end. Just screaming and screaming, and with every new scream Pingüino covered his ears, wincing. "Shhh," Mami said, "Shhh." After a while she was reduced to silent tears, dripping onto her neck, onto her hands wrinkled like an *abuela*'s. This whole time Luis had wanted to kill himself because he thought he had robbed his mother of purpose. And I realized that it was the other way around. He was dead. She was purposeless. Now she would be nothing more than burned nightgowns and wistful cigarettes by the window. Unpicked lemons growing too ripe and falling rotten to the earth. Fruit flies in the yard. The end of things.

Mami held her in her arms. "Who did it?" she said.

Doña Theresa shook her head. Mami offered her a tissue and she took it. "He said he wasn't even supposed to tell me anything. That the police had told him not to. They just wanted me to sit there for the rest of my life wondering where my son had gone, when he'd been killed a couple of doors down, three bullets in the back while running away. They said it was 'random violence,' but I know he was lying. He knew. He knew and he wouldn't tell me. No one saw it happen. Just like with the Hotel Nacional bombings…"

Pingüino and I avoided each other's eyes.

"But Deianeira," Doña Theresa continued, "it doesn't matter how it happened. Because he's dead. Not a person anymore, not my son. Just a pile of flesh somewhere, and it's not fair, because"—she began to sob again—"because he was such a beautiful boy. Even now, I can see him. Picking lemons in the backyard, using the stepladder to get to the highest ones, always talking. He wasn't always like this. Silent and moody. Secretive. He was beautiful. The most beautiful thing. And now no one will ever know."

"He doesn't have to be," Mami whispered. "He doesn't have to be dead. You can keep him beautiful. I think you can keep most things beautiful if you try."

Doña Theresa wiped her eyes. Then she reached into her shirt and pulled out papers. Childlike writing like the letters Doña Paula had spread across our coffee table a few weeks ago.

"Are these the letters?" Mami said.

Doña Theresa nodded. "He was with Fidel. Rodrigo told me this morning. Now we know for sure."

"Mami?" I said. Pingüino was wide-eyed gazing at the letters. "Mami, did you know something?"

"No, not exactly. Doña Theresa and Doña Paula were finding strange letters addressed to Anita and Luis, and they wanted me to help."

"I used to find them beneath the rug on the front porch every couple of days," Doña Theresa said. "I could never figure out what they said because I can't read very well, but I know it was from them. The other rebels. The two boys who came to town a few weeks ago. I saw them leave it from behind the curtains, when they thought I wasn't home. He kept them in an old shoebox. I don't know what to do with them."

We stared at the letters in her hands, the yellowed paper, the writing just visible through the other side.

"Burn them." It was Abuelo who said it. He had his hands clasped in his lap. "That's what you told Doña Paula to do, wasn't it?"

"Burn them," Mami said in agreement. "Now."

The papers burned slowly. Mami went fishing through the kitchen drawers for the blue pack of matches she used for candles when the lights went out. Then we went to the backyard and huddled around the burning pile so no one would see, even though there was no one there to see it. Our next-door neighbours weren't home. We did it on the concrete slab of our backyard beneath the mango trees, the redness of the mangoes shining through the leaves like non-beating hearts, watching like the rest of us.

Doña Theresa didn't want us to read the letters, so Mami folded each piece of paper and lit the edges. There was no wind, but it took a few tries to get the matches working. Every time one of them went out, Mami threw the half-burned stick to the ground and started a new one.

The burning itself surprised me. The flames were barely there. The ashes weren't the way ashes were supposed to be. Not gray and grainy, but large and black. Peeling away like velvet in the breeze. It crumbled so soft it could've been good enough to eat. The heat made us dizzy, drunken almost. We blinked and our eyes felt dry. In the end, all that was left was a small pile of delicate blackness, sifting windless on the concrete.

Later, after Doña Theresa gathered herself and went home, after Abuelo returned to his green chair, after Pingüino trudged to our room to take one last look at the bedroom closet, Mami got out the broom and the dustpan. She held the broom, I knelt on the concrete with the pan, and she swept away every last fleck of darkness from our backyard. But still I felt the flecks hiding. In the dirt of the grass and the cracks in the concrete. I beat the pan against the edge of the trashcan in the kitchen. Out the back window, everything was as still as it had been before Doña Theresa and her purposelessness. The hearts in the trees watched on, as dead as ever.

32.

Esperanza Siempre

When night fell, there was another knock at the door. Mami and I were curled on the couch watching television. Abuelo and Pingüino were in their rooms. Papi opened the door.

"Celia?"

Mami tore her eyes from the television, but it wasn't Celia. It was Tío Rodrigo. The black-and-white police car was parked at the roadside, and Manuel was in the front seat watching our house through the window.

"Rodrigo," Papi said. He eyed Manuel in the police car. "Come in."

Tío Rodrigo stepped across the threshold and saw us on the couch. He took off his hat and rubbed his head.

"What are you doing here?" Papi asked.

"Sebastián, I'm going to have to ask you a couple questions."

"About what?"

"It would be better if we did this outside."

"What is it? Has something gone wrong?"

"Not exactly."

"What do you mean? You got your paycheck, didn't you?"

"Yes, but—"

"They didn't suspect anything, did they?"

"No, it's nothing to do with that."

"Then what is it?"

172

"I really think it might be better if we did this outside."

"Just spit it out."

Tío Rodrigo cleared his throat, "Very well then." He opened the door and made a motion for Manuel to come inside. Manuel lumbered out of the police car with a white box in his hands, and I recognized it. It was the white box with the red shoes. Celia's red shoes. Except the box lay mangled and destroyed in Manuel's hands. Manuel handed the box to Tío Rodrigo.

"Do you know someone named Celia?"

Papi gazed at the white box. "What happened?"

"She's dead, Sebastián."

Papi stared at Tío Rodrigo's face. "What do you mean? How can she be dead?"

"She's just… dead."

Papi's face contorted. He looked around the room helplessly, maybe searching for something to hold onto, but there was nothing. He sat in his own sphere of emptiness.

"Was she the prostitute?" Tío Rodrigo said, and I was surprised at the softness of his voice.

"Don't you—" Papi said, struggling. "Don't you dare. She is so much more than that."

Tío Rodrigo tried again, "Was this the girl you had an affair with?"

"Yes."

"Someone called the police yesterday night because they heard noises coming from this girl's apartment. Manuel and I—we found her body today. The room was a mess. Broken things everywhere. She was on the floor, by the window. Someone had strangled her. And next to her was this shoebox and we found a note in it. From you." Tío Rodrigo took a piece of paper from his pocket and gave it to Papi. He barely glanced at it.

"It was the mobster wasn't it? He sent someone."

"I think so. Yes."

"I've killed her," Papi said.

"No, you haven't," Mami said.

"But I have," Papi said, and he was bewildered with himself. His eyes were shattered just like Miguel's after the Hotel Nacional. He was crying. "I've killed her and it's my fault."

Mami walked over. She hugged him. "Shhh," she said.

"It's all my fault! It's always my fault! Why is it always my fault?"

Mami was silent, stroking his hair. Abuelo and Pingüino had emerged from their bedrooms and they were confused. I didn't bother explaining. Tío Rodrigo said something I didn't catch and then Manuel walked back to the police car with the white box.

"How am I going to live?" Papi said.

"One day at a time," Mami said. "That's how I learned."

"You didn't kill anyone."

"Neither did you."

"But it's my fault."

"It is."

"I tried, Deianeira. I really tried."

"Stop it," Mami said. "Stop it right now. Pitying yourself won't help."

"Will someone tell us what the hell is going on?" Abuelo said.

Papi walked towards the couch and Mami helped him towards it.

"Celia's dead," I said.

"Delita, I'm sorry," Papi said. "I'm so sorry. Pingüino, I'm sorry too."

Pingüino didn't seem sympathetic. "This is stupid."

"Pingüino, be quiet," Mami said.

"How can you even take his side?"

"I'm not. I'm just trying to understand."

"I don't get it. I don't get any of this," Pingüino said.

"You have to try. It doesn't work if you don't try."

"Sebastián," Tío Rodrigo said. "If he's killed her, then we're next."

"We'll leave in the morning," Mami promised.

"You'd better. As for me, I think I'm going to look for an earlier train," Tío Rodrigo said. "I'm sorry, Sebastián," he said to Papi. Then he followed Manuel out the door to his police car.

Papi wasn't listening. He stared at the note in his hands. Mami stared too, and I couldn't tell if she could read it or not. I waited for her to say something, but she didn't.

She got up. "Come on, Pingüino. It's time for bed."

"I don't want to go," Pingüino said.

"I know," Mami said. "I know."

They exited, and left Papi, Abuelo and me in the room.

Abuelo sighed. "I'm going to go pray."

"I thought you didn't pray," I said. "I thought you didn't believe in anything."

"Searching for hope is never a bad thing, especially when you don't believe in it. I would suggest you pray too, Sebastián."

Papi watched us, and crumpled the note into his pocket. "I never said goodbye. I've just realized that. I never said goodbye."

Abuelo stood still. Then he took me by the hand, led me to my room, and tucked me in because no one else would.

33.
The White Rose

Goodbye, Don Rodrigo.

Bang! Bang! Bang!

The three red roses bloomed. Blue and red police lights. The noise of a motor puttering to life, the police car driving away. It made a circle around the body as if it were afraid of waking it, as if it were sleeping with the three roses. In the dirt, the words shone from the pieces of paper like shattered plates, broken moons—"*We write to inform you… unbefitting… la Virgen María… severely scaring her… third offence… We hope this finds you well…*" Shallow breaths. In and out, in and out. Miguel. Pingüino. All three of us stumbling out of the allamanda bush. A leaf in Pingüino's feathery dark hair that resembled Papi's. A yellow flower crumpled and tossed away in Rafi Consuelo's uncut lawn next to the broken refrigerator.

We stumbled across the street. The porch light was on, yellow and bug-infested. On the top step was a half-empty, half-full jug of milk. Droplets of its whiteness glistened on the porch and the steps. It trembled in the grass like dew. I felt bad for Miguel. He'd have to walk by the body a second time to get home. He'd have to circle around the body like his father had. He'd have to try not to look at Luis Rodríguez's face smashed into the pavement, at his dead eyes, his open mouth.

Except he wouldn't. He wouldn't have to do any of those things.

We were on the porch. He was splattered onto the street. We saw it. He got up. He dusted himself off. The bullet holes were non-existent. He stretched, scratched his own back, and when he pulled his hand away there were three red roses. Luis Rodríguez whistled *Guantanamera*. He strolled over as if it wasn't nighttime and he hadn't just been shot. All there was was the tune of it, the words echoing in my head: *Guantanamera, guajira Guantanamera / Guantanamera, guajira Guantanamera / Cultivo una rosa blanca, en junio como en enero...*

It was Christmas. In Havana, the garlands must have been up, the yellow stars and the copper bells. All the streets dressed up. Even Batista would be wearing a star on his head, wrapped up in rounds and rounds of ammunition looped together.

We put our hands out.

"Here you go," Luis said. He handed each of us a rose.

We grabbed them by the stalks and the thorns pricked us, but the centres were all wrong. Each one had a sticky red bullet lodged in the centre, bleeding out. They were warm. They got warmer. They were hot. They seared our fingertips.

"*¡Ay!*" we yelled.

Luis was sad. The three holes in his back bled through his front. His face was pale and dead. "I'm sorry," he said. And it wasn't just him standing there, but it was Papi too. And it was the two strangers and Fidel. And it was Celia and Tío Rodrigo and Batista and whatever the mobster must've looked like. And it was every American who had ever lived, who had ever sat like kings on their continent and thought of the little island people. And even I was there, in the background. Me with my dark blonde hair and my muddy green eyes like my grandmother's.

It was all of them, everyone to be angry at and some of them apologized like Luis, but others didn't. Some stood vacant-eyed and staring like the mobster. Papi was crying and so was Celia, and I saw the finger marks on her throat as if a ghost were choking her. Fidel and Batista eyed each other before Fidel scratched his beard with his gun and Batista adjusted the Christmas star on his head. The two strangers lingered behind Fidel like bodyguards. The other Adela threaded through the crowd as if she were lost or searching for something. I stood before them carrying a burning red rose.

I wanted to throw it back at them. I wanted them to burn. They were intact and I wasn't and it wasn't fair and I could have thrown it back at them, but I didn't.

Instead, I stepped off the porch. Pingüino and Miguel disappeared. I was alone. The lawn was awash in white dew. I knelt in the dirt and dug the earth apart. I felt the mounds beneath my fingernails. I threw in the rose even though its thorns wanted to stay stuck to my fingers. The crowd watched behind me. I pushed the dirt back over the top of it and somehow that was the hardest part, like the earth had gained a thousand pounds, as if each speck were the weight of a boulder.

The ground was silent. Then the rose sprouted through, as white as the dew. The crowd crumbled to ash. The ash blew away and it wasn't gray and grainy, but large and black. Peeling away like velvet in the breeze. Soon the people were a delicate windless pile of black on the street. Then they were gone.

I woke up. It was the morning of leaving and it was dark outside. The dream lent a surrealness to everything, and when I sat up it still felt like a dream. I knelt by my bedside and for the first time, I had nothing to ask. I opened myself. I waited. I waited until my head was so quiet I could hear my own heartbeat. I went into the kitchen and the tile was cool against my feet, the orange of the walls was dim. Through the screen door, I saw Papi's bare back and he was shirtless and unmoving. My eyes stung because I realized what the white roses were all of a sudden, what José Martí had meant all those years ago when he sat in his prison cell and thought of betrayal.

Sometimes people were twisted and human. Sometimes those people were presidents and sometimes they were rebels and sometimes they were family. Sometimes they meant to be horrible and sometimes they didn't. Sometimes I was one of those people too. That was the red-rose way of life. And maybe I would be upset and hate those people for a while, but it shouldn't last forever, it never should. Because I had to absorb the pain and cultivate it within myself until it was something blooming and beautiful and pure. Any old person could be uprooted and angry, but it took a sincere one to bloom even after the heart was torn out still beating. Even after everything, I would do as José Martí did once. I would grow my own white roses. In the dead of night, I planted my first seed. I sat next to Papi on the front porch. He was crying. I leaned against his shoulder and the sun began to rise.

34.
Dale

After that, after we parted, and Papi went to wake Mami, and I went to turn on the lights in our room to wake Pingüino, I was afraid. I had my fingers on the light switch, but I couldn't do it. I remembered the girl in the dream, the other Adela who had threaded through the crowd, stepping between people as if they were trees and she was a person without a name. I looked and I swore I could see her by the darkness of my bedroom window, framed as if in a photograph. She had dark blonde hair and muddy green eyes, but she didn't seem lost anymore. She wore her white sandals like she was going somewhere, like she knew the world was cracked but she was about to set off walking and walking down the road until the light seeped through the fissures of sky above her. She gazed at me and it was almost like she was smiling. *Dale*, she seemed to say. Go on. This is yours.

I took a deep breath.

I turned on the lights.

In the window I saw a reflection, and that was mine too.

35.
Goodbye

When we finally left our tiny blue house in Marianao, the sky was a deep and truthful indigo. The colour of endings, the colour of beginnings. I took one last look at our living room and it had been stripped of soul. The pictures gone from the dresser, the kitchen drawers half-open, all empty. The lights off. Only the big things left behind. The stove and the refrigerator sagging from years of use. The black-and-white television's screen sitting gray, the top of it already gathering dust. The couch and Abuelo's green chair sat as if they belonged in a play, like the first act was about to start, the actors were about to come onstage. There would be a mother and a father and a brother and a sister and maybe even a grandfather. And maybe they would live happily ever after. Or maybe they would all wind up dead. Either way, it was the end of imagining things. It was time to go now. We settled ourselves into Abuelo's car, which was the blue of hard candy. It was a breathless moment before Papi put the keys into the ignition. All five of us had never been in the car together before. Mami and Papi in the front seat. Pingüino, Abuelo, and I jammed into the back. It would be ten hours of this, ten hours of travelling from one side of the island to the other, ten hours for things to sink in once and for all: we were never coming back. The last thing I saw before Papi pulled away from our tiny blue house in Marianao was Abuela's white-and-green curtains through the front window. And I could have sworn that they fluttered a bit, as if somewhere within the house there was a person we had left behind, as if someone were trying to wave goodbye.

Author's Note

Adela Santiago, when she first popped in my head, was in her early twenties. She had dark blonde hair and muddy green eyes, and when the Cuban Revolution came pounding into Havana, she fled to Spain where she waited for a distant lover and learned to sew her own clothing. In other words, she was my grandmother, Catherine Rodríguez, who fled Havana in 1959 and died of Alzheimer's at 60 before I had the chance to know her properly. Catherine had just finished her degree in pharmacy school when she left, and she had got married to one of her professors. When she finally came to the United States, she had to not only learn English, but redo all of her college education. She later became a pharmacist.

Even though Adela's story is no longer my grandmother's, my grandmother played a huge part in how I visualized Cuba in the 1950s. In much the same way that I have a made-up vision of who she was as a person, I also have a made-up vision of what Cuba was. I can't pretend to know what Cuba was like and I can't pretend to know what my grandmother was like. Still, I like to think there are bits of her scattered into this story. She is to me what Adela's grandmother is to her: a ghost floating nearby, smiling bittersweetly. For this reason, I dedicate this book to her.

Acknowledgements

The first person I would like to thank is my mother. Unlike most parents, she stuck by this mess of a novel from the moment it was a collection of vignettes all the way to final edits. She even dealt with me handwriting it in the hotel bathtub while we were on vacation. Needless to say, she's been through a lot.

Second, I would like to thank the various contributors this novel has had. Thank you to Suzanne Supplee for being the most influential mentor I will probably ever have, and for standing by this book (and me) well past the time you were supposed to. Thank you to Barry Goldblatt, Jeff Fan, Rylee Carrillo-Waggoner, Emanuel Poche, Molly St. Ours, Lucy Lopez, and Michael Stewart for reading this book at various stages of its development and for taking the time to love Marianao and its world as much as I did. Thank you also to my publisher and editor Polly Pattullo for devoting so much of herself to this work, for video-chatting me many times at various hours of the morning to discuss line edits, and for generally handling my various neuroses.

Third, I would like to thank CODE, the Bocas Lit Fest, and everyone involved with the Burt Award for Caribbean Young Adult Literature. I have always wanted the opportunity to get this book into the hands of those who were meant to read it, and until this award I wasn't sure that was possible. As a kid, I would have loved to have read a book with people like me at its centre, but those books didn't exist—and if they did, I had no idea how to find them. I am honoured to be given the chance to change that.

Fourth, I would like to thank the rest of my friends and family who have been supportive of my novel-related endeavours in the last four years. These include Dayana Daniyarova, the George Washington Carver Center for Arts and Technology Literary Arts Class of 2016, my father, and my brother, Javier, who giggled himself silly when he found out that Adela's brother's name was Pingüino.

Thank you also to the people who don't know this novel exists. Thank you to my grandmother, Catherine Rodríguez, who died many years ago in a sun-dappled hospital in Miami. Thank you to the Cubans who were brave in the face of Batista's regime and those who are brave now under Castro's. Thank you to José Martí for your belief in white roses. Thank you to anyone else who believes in the art of white roses too.